CARYL PHILLIPS

Crossing the River

Caryl Phillips was born in 1958 in St. Kitts, West
Indies, and went with his family to England that
same year. He was brought up in Leeds and educated
at Oxford. He has written numerous scripts for film,
theater, radio, and television; *The European Tribe*,
a book of nonfiction that won the 1987 Martin
Luther King Memorial Prize; and five novels.

INTERNATIONAL

Books by CARYL PHILLIPS

Crossing the River

CARYL PHILLIPS

Crossing the River

VINTAGE INTERNATIONAL
Vintage Books
A Division of Random House, Inc.
New York

FIRST VINTAGE INTERNATIONAL EDITION, JANUARY 1995

Copyright © 1993 by Caryl Phillips

The Library of Congress has cataloged the Knopf edition as follows:
Phillips, Caryl.
Crossing the river / by Caryl Phillips. — 1st American ed.
p. cm.
ISBN 0-679-40533-X
1. Afro-American families—History—Fiction. 2. Slaves—United
States—Fiction. 3. Afro-Americans—Fiction. 4. Slave traders—
Fiction. I. Title.
PR9272.S263P4728 1994
823.'914—dc20   93-35933
CIP
Vintage ISBN 978-0-679-75794-8

Author photograph © Jillian Edelstein

Manufactured in the United States of America

24

For those who crossed the river

Acknowledgements

I have employed many sources in the
preparation of this novel, but would like
to express my particular obligation to John
Newton's eighteenth-century *Journal of a Slave
Trader*, which furnished me with invaluable
research material for Part III.

I

THE PAGAN COAST

II

WEST

III

CROSSING THE RIVER

IV

SOMEWHERE IN ENGLAND

A desperate foolishness. The crops failed. I sold my children. I remember. I led them (two boys and a girl) along weary paths, until we reached the place where the mud flats are populated with crabs and gulls. *Returned across the bar with the yawl, and prayed a while in the factory chapel.* I watched as they huddled together and stared up at the fort, above which flew a foreign flag. *Stood beneath the white-washed walls of the factory, waiting for the yawl to return and carry me back over the bar.* In the distance stood the ship into whose keep I would soon condemn them. The man and his company were waiting to once again cross the bar. We watched a while. And then approached. *Approached by a quiet fellow.* Three children only. I jettisoned them at this point, where the tributary stumbles and swims out in all directions to meet the sea. *Bought 2 strong man-boys, and a proud girl.* I soiled my hands with cold goods in exchange for their warm flesh. A shameful intercourse. I could feel their eyes upon me. Wondering, *why?* I turned and journeyed back along the same weary paths. *I believe my trade for this voyage has reached its conclusion.* And soon after, the chorus of a common memory began to haunt me.

For two hundred and fifty years I have listened to the many-tongued chorus. And occasionally, among the sundry restless voices, I have discovered those of my own children. My Nash. My Martha. My Travis. Their lives fractured. Sinking hopeful roots into difficult soil. For two hundred and fifty years I have longed to tell them: Children, I am your father. I love you. But understand. There are no paths in water. No signposts. There is no return. To a land trampled by the muddy boots of others. To a people encouraged to war among themselves. To a father consumed with guilt. You are beyond. Broken-off, like limbs from a tree. But not lost, for you carry within your bodies the seeds of new trees. Sinking your hopeful roots into difficult soil. And I, who spurned you, can blame only myself for my present misery. For two hundred and fifty years I have waited patiently for the wind to rise on the far bank of the river. For the drum to pound across the water. For the chorus to swell. Only then, if I listen closely, can I rediscover my lost children. A brief, painful communion. A desperate foolishness. The crops failed. I sold my children.

I

The Pagan Coast

The news reached him after dinner. A well-liveried domestic entered the drawing-room, bowed and thrust forward a silver tray on top of which sat an envelope. Edward seized the letter and dismissed the servant with an elegant flick of his wrist. He levered himself upright and began to read. It was true. Nash Williams, sent to Liberia under the auspices of the American Colonization Society, having undergone a rigorous program of Christian education, and being of sound moral character, had disappeared from the known world. After seven difficult years in Liberia, in which he had worked with unswerving application to his own and his God's tasks, in which he had apparently won the respect not only of the African natives, but of the free colored men from America, and of the few whites in the inhospitable clime, after seven long years this former bondsman who had been an inspiration to priests and educators alike was nowhere to be found. The worst was feared.

Nash Williams was a teacher of remarkable gifts. He was a man who, in a country in which fewer than two hundred heathens had been converted in almost twenty years, could lay claim to being responsible for at least fifty of the successes that were reported back to America. The reputation of his mission school was legendary, a fact all the more remarkable given the isolated position it occupied near the known head of the Saint Paul's River. The few letters he had sent back to his master, whilst full of the usual childish requests for tools, seeds, money and other necessities of life, positively bristled with the spirit of faith, courage and purpose. Then, a little under a year ago, and at the same time as a saddened Edward was mourning the loss of his wife, Nash Williams had conveyed, by means of an intermediary, an abrupt message making it plain that he had no desire ever to hear again from his former master, and informing him that his own communications would now cease. A disturbed and worried Edward, judging it best, at this juncture, not to communicate directly with Nash, had word and money sent by means of a packet out of New York that Madison Williams, an older and somewhat haughty former bondsman, should immediately journey from his place of abode in Monrovia and secure news of Nash's whereabouts and, if possible, his general state of health. Madison had, at an earlier time, borne Nash some feelings of ill-will, having reasoned, and to some degree correctly, that his master's affection for himself had been usurped by this younger interloper. But Edward trusted that the passage of time, and a change of climate, would have healed these old wounds, and that Madison would not resent the task with which he was now being entrusted. However, the letter before Edward bore the disturbing news of Madison's expedition. Not only had Madison failed to locate Nash, but he had been blocked at every turn by native intransigence, their crude vulgarity sometimes taking the form of aggression. The details set forth in Madison's sad letter let it be known that he considered himself fortunate to have escaped with his life intact.

Not that the American Colonization Society was ignorant of the dangers that would accompany their policy of attempting to repatriate former slaves on the west coast of Africa. This was, after all, a continent belonging to the native African, and to nobody else. But they hoped that the natives would see reason, and that the prospect of welcoming home their lost children might help to overcome any unpleasant cultural estrangement that the African heathens might temporarily experience. The American Colonization Society was sure that benefits would accrue to both nations. America would be removing a cause of increasing social stress, and Africa would be civilized by the return of her descendants, who were now blessed with rational Christian minds. And so on January 31st, 1820, the ship *Elizabeth* left New York for the west coast of Africa on what was to be the American Colonization Society's inaugural voyage. Some weeks later, eighty-six former slaves, half of whose number were women and children, arrived unsuccessfully in the British territory of Sierra Leone. Sadly, a mysterious malady, later understood to be malaria, soon dispatched all but a fortunate few of this initial batch of pioneers. Two years later, in 1822, a second and more successful expedition deposited settlers on the Grain Coast, at the part of West Africa that would soon become known as Liberia.

Being chosen for colonization was regarded by most slaves and their masters as reward for faithful service. A skilled worker, who was also a converted Christian with a sound moral base, was considered a prime candidate. But reports from early settlers told stories of great hardships. The initial work of clearing the bush, constructing shelters and building fortifications against native attacks resulted in a heavy toll of life. The wet and miserable climate, which between April and November could produce over two hundred inches of rain, ushered many to an early grave. From December through until March, the poor, unfortunate newcomers, having survived the floods, now labored in unbearably high temperatures, and endured a humidity of stifling proportions. But it was the African fever, or malaria, which most affected the lives of the settlers. The severe chills, producing a sensation of cold as fearful as any American winter, and the accompanying delusions which infected the imagination, combined to introduce a deep misery. No longer were these unfortunate creatures pioneering in the welcoming bosom of their native land, with a clear blue sky for a roof and a fertile soil beneath their dusty feet. They were being tossed upon the stormy seas of fever, and when the storm diminished many found they had been driven clear out of this mortal world.

By the second decade of emigration, very little had changed. Pioneers still arrived, their innocent faces etched with a passionate desire to do God's work, but sadly they soon found themselves unable successfully to weather the twelve-month seasoning period, and friends and relatives were called upon to be the messengers of melancholy intelligence to those they had left behind in America. One who arrived in this period, and one of those most determined to survive and pursue the task that he had been prepared for, was Nash Williams. Neither climate nor native confrontation, disease nor hardship of any manner would deflect him from his proper purpose. Word soon reached his former master that on many occasions he had to be prevailed upon in the harshest terms to cease working in the rain in the best interests of his health. On receiving this news Edward Williams felt moved secretly to reach for his pen and address the first of his two letters to his former slave. A portion of this first letter contained the following words of wisdom:

Before you left America, I reminded you of the sacrifices that our good Lord Jesus Christ made for us all, and urged you to consider the situation of Christianity in this new country that you inhabit. You were kind enough not only to dwell upon my words, but to convey back to me in the form of a letter information as to the unlettered and heathen state of the masses. For this both my good wife, Amelia, and myself are grateful. Such information will no doubt prove vital to those slaves whom we are now preparing, in order that they might one day join you on the pagan coast. However, I am somewhat dismayed to hear (from a source you will no doubt guess) about your continued insistence upon attempting to carry out tasks, without recourse to aid from other fellows, that would strain five men, both physically and mentally, either Christian or native. Christ's sacrifices were many, but surely your acquaintance with the Good Book will have revealed to you that they were calculated. Even He could not do everything in one day. You are fortunate in being blessed with a *fair* mind and strong body and (although I say so myself) doubly fortunate in that your former master was of a progressive persuasion. Do not disappoint me, or yourself, by falling short of the high standards that you have already set yourself. Only yesterday the children gathered about Amelia and asked after your well-being, and then said prayers for you. Our whole experiment depends greatly upon your success. Your resolve may be firm, but we are all flesh and blood. I hope that you understand that I speak to you in order to assist in your development. May I suggest that you study the Good Book for further guidance.

Sadly, this letter was uncovered by Edward's wife, Amelia, and not conveyed. However, never again did Edward receive intelligence that his former bondsman Nash had either disobeyed his instruction, put himself in unnecessary mortal danger, or done anything that might lead Edward once more to consider reaching for the pen and composing lines of disapproval.

In 1841, having received the letter from his former slave Madison, and having fully digested its discomfiting contents, Edward Williams rose from his chair in the drawing-room and immediately set about making plans to journey to Liberia in order that he might determine for himself what had befallen the virtuous Nash. His plan was to travel alone by the first ship that was sailing for the coast, and he foresaw no reason for there to be a delay of any kind. Being now a widower, he would have to endure neither harsh nor reproachful words from his lady wife, Amelia, who would no doubt have been gravely suspicious of the motives which lay behind his projected expedition. At first, and much to Edward's surprise, the idea of this scheme did not win the consent of the officials of the American Colonization Society. Though full of admiration for the enthusiasm of Edward Williams, and sympathetic to the ardor he continued to display towards his black charges, they were at pains to point up to him the many dangers to which he might unwittingly be exposing himself. Edward persisted in his communications with them, and eventually, but only after much altercation, they chose to relent their opposition and grant cautious support. At first they had insisted that the mysterious disappearance of a single settler was something they could reasonably expect to occur on a regular basis. Such was the peril of dispatching good men to heathen shores at the edge of civilization, and encouraging them to make this African land their home. But Edward had argued that to abandon men as remarkable as Nash could only reflect adversely on the future of the Society. He reminded the Society that, on his own initiative, he had borne the not inconsiderable expense of sending this man to college in Virginia, in order that he might be thoroughly prepared and trained for the life of a missionary. And further, he had encouraged all of his former slaves, including Nash, to avoid Monrovia, and like wind-driven seeds to scatter themselves about the land in the hope that there might be a widespread distribution of the message of the Lord. Only Nash had heeded his words. He had settled up-river in native country, having taken to his bosom a good Christian wife from Georgia, one Sally Travis, now deceased. Edward reminded the Society that, together with his wife, Nash had operated the most successful of the mission schools for natives. In fact, Edward had reminded them of this fact at every possible juncture, for, according to his closely argued deposition, this was not simply the sacrifice of one missionary, a victim of untreated fever or ill-advised wanderings into the interior. Edward was adamant that the disappearance of Nash could signal a humiliating defeat for the Society's ideals as a whole, and he was determined to reach the territory of Liberia and investigate matters with his own eyes. Finally, the American Colonization Society, having listened with patience, came to realize that indeed there was more virtue in assisting Edward Williams than in impeding him.

It was customary at this time to set sail from Virginia or New York, but Edward had determined to leave on the first available ship, irrespective of its port of departure. He spread before himself a map of the known world, and stared at the inelegant shape of Africa, which stood like a dark, immovable shadow between his own beloved America and the exotic spectacle of India and the countries and islands of the Orient. He would travel for an undetermined length of time, although he had been led to believe that twenty-eight days was not at all unusual for such a journey. Fortunately, he was already armed with some knowledge of what rigors he might reasonably expect to face, both on the passage and after arrival, through the evidence of those letters from his former slaves which Amelia had permitted him to peruse. They spoke of problems and difficulties which would inevitably tax the health of a man of Edward's fragile constitution, but common sense and restraint would be his guides.

Born in 1780, the son of a wealthy tobacco planter, Edward had inherited his father's estate in his twenty-ninth year, and with it the sum total of three hundred slaves. A rich man of unrivalled wealth, he could simply have luxuriated himself and slipped quietly into a premature retirement, but he also inherited from his father an aversion to the system which had allowed his fortunes to multiply. Edward soon took the unusual initiative of encouraging his slaves to acquire the generally forbidden arts of reading and writing. When, some years after his windfall of slaves, he became aware of the formation of the American Colonization Society, this seemed an ideal opportunity to divest himself of the burden, or at least some part of the burden, of being a slave-owner, a title which ran contrary to his Christian beliefs. His wife, though initially not sharing fully in his unusually philanthropic fervor, had slowly come to tolerate the strange behavior and desires of her husband. But, sadly, she was no more. And now the chief player in his game, the most successful of his Christian blacks, was lost somewhere on the dismal coastline of Africa. Day and night a troubled Edward mused over Nash. Had that dark face, charged with belief and propriety, been somehow changed in the humid and barbarous climate? He could not believe that Africa could have distorted Nash's faith, and encouraged him to turn his back on his God. And why now, after all these years of patience, had he suddenly chosen to break off with his former master? This troubling conundrum, which each night kept Edward awake and tossing first this way and then that, threatened to tear apart his very soul. He knew that he had little choice but to travel to Liberia, not simply to discover the truth surrounding the fate of his Nash, but in order to confirm that his life's work, and more importantly his own life, had been of some worth.

On the evening of November 3rd, 1841, the *Mercury* set sail out of New York harbor. On deck, Edward Williams knelt and prayed both for the soul of his dearly departed Amelia, and for the success of the journey he was embarking upon. As they passed out beyond the stillness of the river and into the sea, he leaned over the rail and watched his beloved America recede from view and eventually vanish behind the horizon. Sadly, within a day of their departure, thick black clouds appeared overhead and they hit upon a terrible storm in which the ceaseless rain cascaded down from a perpetually dark sky. Edward remained below and listened through the planks to the moaning of his fellow passengers, a parcel of Louisiana blacks headed for the coast, who lay about the boards stricken into various stages of mortality. They were a week out of New York, and the storm had still not abated, when the mast came crashing down. The sailors were men of experience, but for some time it appeared as though the ship would have to be abandoned to the wind and waves, for there seemed to be no end to this tempest. All who were able were summoned on deck to help repair the ailing vessel, but by this time Edward had contracted the fever and was unable to bestir himself in any way. He lay below and listened to the painful creaking and straining of the wood, as the squalls grew ever more violent. Mercifully, midway through the second week, the storm finally blew itself out, but soon after the true and unbearable force of the sun's heat was upon them. Long, sunstruck afternoons assailed the ship, the sky forever clear and without even the slightest stain of a cloud, the air still and bereft of any breeze that might flutter a sail or distort the mirror of the sea. The journey was now in danger of becoming prolonged past the supply of food and, more crucially, water. Sadly, despite the efforts of the ship's surgeon, Edward's ghastly condition, his body roaring with fever, showed no sign of improving. The Captain, a man renowned for his sagacity, resigned himself to the inevitable loss of his most illustrious passenger.

At last, on the evening of December 14th, 1841, the *Mercury* limped into the harbor at the British settlement of Freetown, Sierra Leone, the Captain having thought it politic to acquire fresh supplies and immediate medical help for those, like Edward, who lay between life and death. Natives came on board and bore Edward, perspiration flowing down his forehead, his body racked with chills and fever, into a crudely constructed rowing boat. Through the haze of illness Edward could hear, in fact almost taste, the sea, which stretched out all around him, melancholy and still. By straining his half-closed eyes, it was possible for him to discern the shoreline, where torches burned in the moonless dusk. The short journey seemed interminable, and was made worse by the descent of a thick mist which soon turned into a light rain. On reaching Freetown, Edward was clumsily lifted on to a rudimentary cart that was to be pulled by a solitary mule. The black driver yelled at the dispirited beast, and Edward felt the cart lurch, the wheels spin idly in the mud, but the whole contraption remained painfully static. After much bellowing and inconvenience to Edward, he was eventually, by these impossible means, transported to a mission hospital whose only virtue appeared to be the number of white faces which inhabited this otherwise insanitary place. Here Edward lingered for some days, his hand in the hand of his God, until the tide turned and washed him back upon the shores of this earth.

After a week, in which his body grew accustomed to solid foods, and in which he learned how to walk again without aid, Edward was impatient to commence upon the final measure of his journey. It was at this juncture that the British doctor informed him that his ship, the *Mercury*, had set sail without waiting for those passengers who had been discharged. It appeared that some trading dispute had broken out between Sierra Leone and Liberia, which meant that all exchange, commercial or otherwise, between the two territories had, for the time being, been suspended. Apparently, the *Mercury* was not welcome in Sierra Leone as long as she flew openly and with pride the American flag. Edward felt desperate, and made immediate and hourly cross-examination of the doctor as to how he might reach Liberia. He was keen to impress upon this man the seriousness of his intent, but the doctor was powerless to help beyond offering up the suggestion that either Edward attempt the passage overland, or he wait in Sierra Leone for this diplomatic squabble to subside. In response to Edward's enquiries as to the general health of the Liberian experiment, the doctor simply shrugged his shoulders. What could he say? He had never been to Liberia, but neither would he want to travel there. Here, in the Crown Colony of Sierra Leone, he was British. There he would be nothing. He touched Edward lightly on the arm, in that manner which doctors soon accustom themselves to in order that they might assuage the fears of their patients. His advice was to wait. He assured Edward that these disputes tended to be short-lived. There was little to be gained by worrying excessively.

Monrovia, Liberia
September 11th, 1834

Dear Beloved Benefactor,

I am exceedingly happy to take up my pen and embrace this precious opportunity of addressing you a few lines. I trust that God in His mercy will spare you to read these words and many more. My family and I were blessed with a safe and prosperous passage over the briny deep, and delivered safely to this African land. Accordingly, I thank God that I remain alive to have the pleasure of writing to you from distant shores. Though we are separated by wide waters and steep mountains, you, my dear father, are forever with me in my mind. That we were only seventeen days at sea speaks of the fine weather that we were fortunate enough to have bestowed upon us. Further, the ship happily improved her numbers, for there was one birth at sea. This is the first opportunity I have had to send to you a humble communication since our arrival here. I do so in the hope that my crude lines might find both yourself and your wife in fine health, thanks be to God. We are all well, with the exception of young York, upon whom the sea-sickness vented itself with uncommon fury, and whose childish body has yet to recover equilibrium. Fortunately, my wife Sally is of a more rigorous constitution and dutifully nurses him while I attend to more pressing matters. Among the other emigrants of our ship with whom you will be familiar, only old Nancy and big Mabel were ill at ease on the sea. The rest are somewhat well, and earnestly salute your noble person, although many are now touched up with the African fever.

Galloway Williams is dead. He died only a day since. His wife, Constance, who arrived in this country aboard the same packet as myself, was only last week delivered of a fine son, but alas the Lord saw it fit to take the child. He could not have taken it at a better time, the child being but an infant, but He soon after took to Him Constance also, to be with the child, and now Galloway to afford his wife some support in the hereafter. The Lord giveth and the Lord taketh, blessed be the name of the Lord. The burden you placed upon us of repeating the Ten Commandments, which we considered a form of punishment, has proved of the utmost importance in meeting the pain of these trying times. As a father you cared for us, and we hope that the Lord will reward you for your kindness.

Liberia is a fine place to live in. I was at first astonished to see the bushes that grow in the streets, and the boldness of the nature all about, but my person is now accustomed to these strange sights. Thank God I have been spared to reach here in good health and by His permission do still enjoy it. The town of Monrovia is well-watered and timbered, and if a person could have a little capital he would do very well. A colored person can enjoy his liberty in this place, for there exists no prejudice of color and every man is free and equal. Although, dear father, I am greatly desirous of seeing you again before we leave this world, I doubt if I shall ever consent to return again to America. Liberia, the beautiful land of my forefathers, is a place where persons of color may enjoy their freedom. It is the home for our race, and a country in which industry and perseverance are required to make a man happy and wealthy. Its laws are founded upon justice and equality, and here we may sit under the palm tree and enjoy the same privileges as our white brethren in America. Liberia is the star in the East for the free colored man. It is truly our only home.

Sadly, there is amongst some emigrants a tendency for lying about and doing nothing. True, it is very hot hereabouts, but after the industrious man achieves acclimatization, there is no excuse for not applying himself with unwearied dedication. Those who won't work and who get along by stealing are becoming something like the natives.

18

Of the money you lodged for me with Mr Gray, I have not seen one cent of it as the *gentleman* denies all knowledge of the matter. Why he does so I cannot say, but it is so. I informed him that as I am determined to obey your instructions and proceed to the country in order that I might establish a school, I shall require capital. He countered with the knowledge that it would be a deathly and ruinous undertaking to go up there, the native population being uncivilized so that during sickness with fever I would most certainly be robbed of whatever articles of value I might possess. Indeed, the scantiness of the Christian population beyond Monrovia is somewhat surprising, but I am resolved to lead by example and carry the word of God to the heathens.

My resolution has occasioned something of a rift to develop between my good wife, Sally, and myself. She remains steadfast in her belief that the Lord, having blessed me with a reasonable portion of health, will surely regard the exposing of my person to the rigors of the country as both eccentric and foolish. Her concern was initiated by the most recent bleeding from the nose that I suffered. The climate agrees with my health in many respects, but in some respects it does not. This rainy season that we presently endure will, I fear, eventually prove the most injurious portion of the year with reference to my constitution. I have already suffered several bleeding attacks, but this most recent one, which commenced shortly before noon last Sabbath morning, lasted two full hours. It then ceased its red passage, only to recommence at six in the evening, whereupon it determined to set its course clear through until midnight. Sally offered up a volley of prayers to Him that orders all things to His own glory, and clearly He set a favorable ear to her pleading, for the discharge and discomfort soon ceased their labors.

Father, some emigrants hereabouts, having previously embraced religion and displayed the patience necessary to resist the temptation of the evil one, now dance to the discordant tune of drunkenness. I am, however, happy to report that not only my wife but those of our immediate acquaintance remain steadfast in our beliefs. I have attended worship at every opportunity, and find the people very friendly, as does my wife. Her anxieties concerning our impending journey into the interior merely reflect her unease upon receiving alarming stories of the primitive state of affairs beyond this Monrovia. Rest assured, dear father, for she remains a true Christian.

Please give my true love to all my friends, and urge them to conduct themselves in such a manner that they might reasonably expect to meet me in Heaven, that is if I am not fortunate once again to lay eyes upon them in this world. In particular, Aunt Sophie, George, Hannah, Peter Thornton, Fanny Gray, Aggy and Charlotte, Miss Mathilda Danford, Henry, Randolph and Nancy. Above all, please give my love to my dear mother, but you who have done more for me than natural father, or any other, must keep the greater portion of my affections for yourself. Please read what follows in the presence of all your servants so that they might know from one who is free, and in no manner in bondage, thus in no way obligated to express such sentiments, what quality of master they are blessed with: –

There are those servants who, having served their master for more than fifty years, are not rewarded with their liberty, but are instead sold at auction to the highest bidder. How good the Almighty is to have blessed you with such a master as this, for there is not another under Heaven such as your master. I have found since my arrival in Africa that many of your master's ways and fashions, burdensome though they were while in America, have served to form the basis of my character and have enabled me to survive this seasoning period with relative ease. Under his tutelage my understanding has been enlightened, so I beg of you servants to pay attention, attend school, and seize the opportunity to learn, for not all masters are so inclined to place the wisdom and good sense of the Bible at the disposal of their colored property.

And now to you, dear Father. If they should refuse to attend school or heed your words, you must punish them, whether young or old, for as I have already observed in these parts, too much pleasure brings on sin and ruin. I humbly remind you once more that you should convey my love to my own dear mother, who has been happy in your service for the greater part of her ancient life. Should she be visited by a change of heart, and desire to live out her final years in the bosom of Africa, or should she simply move past useful labor, I trust that despite her unlettered state you would allow her liberty to undertake such a journey. Dear father, I have recently read again the very kind letter you gave me as I set out for college some years ago. It gives me more pleasure than I can express to think that I have one such as you as both advisor and friend, and as I pursue my calling of teacher, I pray that the Lord will not abandon me, for without Him we are nothing and can do nothing. I praise His holy name that I was fortunate enough to be born in a Christian country, amongst Christian parents and friends, and that you were kind enough to take me, a foolish child, from my parents and bring me up in your own dwelling as something more akin to son than servant. Truth and honesty is great capital, and you instilled such values in my person at an early age, for which I am eternally grateful to you and my Creator. Had I been permitted simply to run about, I would today be dwelling in the same robes of ignorance which drape the shoulders of my fellow blacks. Words cannot express my gratitude for the care you displayed towards me during my younger days, for as the Scripture says, train up a child in the way he should go, and when he is old he will not depart from it. I am ever hopeful that we might see each other's faces again in the flesh, but if the Lord has ordained it otherwise, then I trust that we shall be amongst that number that John saw surrounding the Throne of the Lamb, where sorrow, pain and death are neither felt nor feared no more.

I look up to you as a son to a kind father and will ever expect assistance as long as we hear from each other.

Presently I stand in need of help from you by the first chance, for I have not received one cent from your man, and the Society agents hereabouts seem determined to clasp what little there is to their own bosoms. Will you be so kind as to send me some mustard seed and some flax seed for stomach complaint? Father, will you please send me a pair of spectacles for my own use, and a further pair for my wife, Sally? I am very much in want of clothing; you may send some coarse cloth, and shoes. Further, my wife begs of you a spinning wheel and cards to keep her employed. I plead with you, sir, on behalf of myself, to aid us. The amount of four to five hundred dollars would be of little consequence to a man such as yourself, but in this hard country it can overnight alter a man's fortunes. Anything further that you choose to send, whether dry goods or provisions, will be very acceptable, for this is no different from other new countries. Mr John Sawyer asks if you would be so kind as to send a pair of drum heads. He says he entrusted them to the care of the Captain, but they got wet and the mice made a hole in them. This tale is his own.

I wish you to be so kind as to try to remember my best regards to all enquiring friends. You might remind them to try and serve the Lord, in the hope that He might provide a way for them to reach these lands of civil and religious privileges. At present I have no more to say about myself which can be interesting to you. So, dear sir, receive the kindest wishes of this humble servant. I bid you adieu and do remain your most sincere and affectionate son until death. Dear Father, I trust that the Lord will continue to guard and protect you from all harm and dangers in this sinful world. My prayer to God is that He will bless and preserve you long in life, and at death – having finished your course and performed the work assigned to you – receive you into Heaven where you may sit at the right of God. I hope we shall meet there to part no more. Your affectionate son.

Nash Williams

Saint Paul's River, Liberia
October 22nd, 1835

My Dear Father,

This letter leaves me in not a good state of health. I have had the fever, but now embrace the present opportunity of writing a few lines, my intention being to forward them to you by means of the Liberia packet which sails in a few days. I sincerely hope that my letter might find yourself and your wife in better circumstances than those which presently assault my person. It is to be hoped that you may live a long number of years, blessed by the Lord in many ways, and do more good on earth.

I am no longer of Monrovia, having relocated into the heart of the country. Before I left that place I wrote to you on two occasions by Mr Andrews, and once more directly, but I suppose my communication was transmitted into several hands and you did not get it, which is often the way. You know best. I am unable to give you intelligence as to the progress of others for we live so far apart, some few in this direction, but most in the capital town. I am truly now a pioneer of sorts. I am striving to do all the good I can amongst these natives, who form a most dominant majority. To this end I am even speaking a little of their crude dialect, which is very hard to learn. I can, if truth be told, understand it better than I can speak it, but with practice this state of affairs will regulate itself. Since receiving the land, I have not had the opportunity of doing much, but I have made some significant improvements. The first of these has involved the construction of a primitive school building under the watchful supervision of myself. The natives worked with glee, and now this heathen village has a mission school where I am able to instruct in writing intelligibly, in the Bible, in arithmetic, and in geography. I labor purposefully as a teacher in the hope that these heathens may one day soon become lettered. Come Sabbath, our school is transformed, by the simple method of my decree, into a small Baptist church where I preach and provide the multitudes with the opportunity of hearing the Gospel.

The second of my significant improvements relates to efforts to till the soil. I have made a start of farming, and cleared some fifteen to twenty acres of my land, and have planted it down with coffee trees, and cotton, and potatoes, and cassava, and much more kinds of plants such as this Africa affords. I have been led to understand that this land is exceedingly rich, and will eventually yield up everything in abundance. That is, if the seed is properly planted, and taken care of by keeping it clear of grass and weeds. With common industry, a man can raise more of everything than he can use, and have much to sell besides. I soon hope to be in the prosperous situation where I might expect to exchange the results of my labors upon the land for foreign produce. I am led to believe that a little of this trading occurs in Monrovia, but I am now, for good or ill, a man of the country. I will enclose with this letter some paw-paw seeds which are dried in ashes. Perhaps they are cured incorrectly. If they do not produce the required result, I shall procure a variety, fix them as they should be, and forward them by the next chance.

I will share with you a few words about the animals in this place. I have been visited by a cunning leopard in the past few days, who has taken off with both goats and hogs, two of each if my count is correct. I watched out for this creature but could never see him. Leopards often visit Monrovia, where they walk the streets at night committing great depredations. Here, far removed from what passes as civilization, their task is made considerably easier. Recently, I killed a snake of nine feet in length, and the proud possessor of a tremendous girth. He was black and red in color and basking on the margin of the river with an air of unfettered superiority. In addition, we have quite a variety of handsome birds, although their names still elude me.

As you know, an industrious man who is free from debt of any kind can live in tolerable comfort, yet when a man becomes involved in debt, whether it be his fault or not, he often suffers much from this circumstance. A little aid from you, dear Father, would do me much good at this time. 'Giving doth not impoverish.' I would be glad to plague you a little to see if you would send me out some trade goods that I might in the due passage of time answer with coffee, ginger, arrowroot and other materials that I will presently crop from my land. Good white shirting, shoes, stockings, tobacco, flour, port, mackerels, molasses, sugar, and a small flitch of bacon and other little trifles as you find convenient to send. Though cotton is raised in this country, there is at present not so much as to be able to manufacture clothes. If you could send some good strong cloth in order that shirts, pantaloons and other clothes be made available for the modesty of the natives hereabouts, I should be most grateful. A half-keg of 10d nails and a half-keg of 4d nails would be very acceptable. I also need some borax but cannot get it in this country. Please mark the box with my full name and direct it to the Saint Paul's River settlement, where full knowledge and appreciation of my Christian work grows with each merciful day.

Since the passing of my wife and child, my wants are few, and of course they are easily supplied in this land of darkness. I have nothing to fear. America is, according to my memory, a land of milk and honey, where people are not easily satisfied. Things that seemed to me then to hold so much value are now, in this new country, and in my new circumstances, without value. All that I now wish for is enough to give me comfort and some small happiness whilst I dwell in this world, for I have learned, by means of sad experience, and by close study of the Scripture, that we carry nothing out of this world when we go hence. In addition to my latest bout with the African fever, I have also a complaint in the hip which you may remember occurred before I left America as a consequence of being thrown from an unruly horse. I hope to meet in Heaven with my dearly departed Sally and my only boy, York, and thereafter dwell with them for ever. This blessed hope, to meet where there will be no further trouble, no vainglorious toil, no more parting, and to sing the praises of God and the Lamb for ever and ever! Surely the religion of Christ is my greatest comfort in this dark world. I pray that the Lord may bless, protect and defend you through life by his unerring counsel, and that when the voyage of life is over and He has no more for you to do on earth, He will take you to live with Him in glory.

My glorious asylum in Liberia remains under the protection of a wise God, who promises to be a God of all nations, provided they obey and dutifully serve Him. Although a country with some inconveniences, there remain many privileges to be enjoyed, for any man can live here that will work, although the quality of man that is these days choosing to make this new country his home leaves me with some cause for concern. Two months past I paid a visit to Monrovia to try to force the hand of that scoundrel who clings to what is rightfully mine. There I encountered others of a similar mind to Mr Gray, unchristian in their behavior and vulgar in their demeanor, whose only visible occupation seemed to be to prey upon poor unfortunate creatures such as myself. True, there are many fine, charitable societies abounding in Monrovia, and churches of all denominations, but I fear that unless the agents of the Society exercise a firmer grip, the affairs of this young country might yet slide out of course. I chanced to spend a part of one morning in conversation with Ellis Thornton Williams, of whom you no doubt have fond memory. You will be pleased to hear report that he has settled in the country to the north of our capital town, and cleared land and planted a fine crop of rice, corn and cassavas. He has on his farm about two dozen Congo boys, the greater number of them having been rescued from the dungeons of a slaver by a British man-of-war. He has very near ninety acres under cultivation, is blessed with a brace of fine sons, and is in tolerably fine health. This chance meeting served to lift my spirits, for by this time I was convinced that the character of all our Monrovian people of color was rotting in this African heat. My conclusion is that a man's spirit and wholesomeness is more pleasantly watered and nourished among the heathen natives of the country, for there one can daily observe the evidence of Christian work which marks out the superiority of the American life over the African.

Now a few words to my dear beloved mother which I trust you will be kind enough to read to her:–

Dear Mother, your advice to me when a child remains in my breast as fresh and as full of wisdom as the day you delivered it. I pray that God will spare you to behold your son's face once more. I am sorry to inform you of the death of Solomon Charles, whom I believe was known to you in earlier times. Beyond this sad occurrence, there is little further in the way of news. When Sally was asked by your son, 'How stands it between thee and thy God?' her answer was, 'All is clear. I am willing to go.' Yes, these were her words, but two days before her death. Mother, how stands it with Uncle Daniel? Is he still living, or should I expect to meet him in Heaven? Since I have been in this country, I have been stricken with the African fever on many occasions. I am still not full with health, but I am somewhat improved. Yesterday I moved amongst the natives who labor about my land. They are good workers, although they require a stern and watchful supervision. Now dear mother, I must come to a close in the knowledge that God and Mr Edward Williams will take care of you. Give my respects to all, white and black. I remain your affectionate son, Nash Williams.

Dear Father, I wish you to be so kind as to remember my best respects to my old fellow servants, and any other enquiring friends. Hoping that they will behave themselves to you. If they fail to do so, you must remind them of the many kindnesses that you have showered upon my humble person. You are ever present in my affections. Perhaps you might dispatch some books for my school. Valuable readers are a most necessary part of my mission. Also, I would be glad to learn my true age. When I write again I shall try and send you some curiosities. I subscribe myself a servant of God, and the friend of my fellow men. As this letter will reach you, I hope, by Christmas, I will conclude by wishing your good lady wife and yourself a Merry Christmas, and sincerely hope that you both enjoy many more. Farewell, dear sir, and receive the kindest wishes of your humble servant and affectionate son.

Nash Williams

Saint Paul's River, Liberia
March 10th, 1839

My Dear Father,

I am taking this favorable opportunity of writing a few
hasty lines in the hope that they might be conveyed to you
by the departure of the vessel *Mathilda* which will presently
leave these shores for America. Your letter reached me on
Feb. 5th, and was read with great joy. I declaimed it aloud
to the people here and its kind contents caused some tears to
flow. I am sad to learn that your brother has been called to
his long and happy home, but reassured by the information
that his was only a short illness of ten to twelve hours. That
your good lady wife, Amelia, still enjoys rude health must
be a great blessing to you. I would be happy if you could
give her my regards, and inform her that there are many
in this dark country of Liberia for whom she represents the
highest achievement in womankind.

Why, dear Father, you chose to ignore my previous
letters, you do not indicate. I must assume that this
represents your either not receiving them, or your finding
their contents so ignorant and poor in expression that you
rightly deemed them unworthy of response. Whatever your
reasoning, I am overjoyed to receive news of my friends
and family, with the one obvious exception. What news
for yourself? Mr Lambert has taken an Alabama woman
by the name of Bertha, and her son Prince, to live with him
in his brick house in Monrovia. It seems he is doing well in
business, although this illiterate woman chooses to behave
herself improperly. And perhaps you have already heard,
by means of some other source, that old brother Taylor
and sister Nancy have both lost all religion. The former
has in addition turned out to be a great and scandalous
drunkard. He is accused of habitual intoxication, much
nocturnal revelling, lewdness, and in fact everything that

characterizes the immoral man. You may correctly deduce from the above that I have severed all connections with this man. They say that his decline was occasioned by the misfortune of losing his youngest son to a sore mouth.

Of the two new arrivants that you recommended to my care, first good news and then sad. Young Solomon Williams is now comfortably situated here with us. He is working the fields for seventy-five cents a day in the hope that he might one day purchase some farmer's tools to commence farming for himself. When he first approached my presence, I had no knowledge of him, save the name he bore. After a little discourse I recognized the fellow. At first he tested his freedom, and acted like a young horse out of the stable, but I soon reined him in. He is now learning his trade finely, and is upon the whole a very proper boy. He suits me well, and may one day (if he continues in a sober fashion) make a useful man for our young country. Of the second arrivant, only sad news. After surviving a difficult voyage of forty-nine days, marred by an outbreak of smallpox which took the lives of some thirty persons, he soon departed, but his end was peace. He was taken sick on a Monday and his end was Wednesday. His illness, though severe, was of only three days' duration when it terminated fatally, his chief complaint being of a pain in the head. He lay in Monrovia and, according to sources, the Reverend visited him each day, and questioned him concerning his soul's salvation, and whether the way from earth to glory was clear or not, to which he would always answer the same, that his hopes were anchored in Jesus Christ. He was, come Wednesday, perfectly sensible of his death as he fell asleep in Jesus's arms, never more to have earthly communion with our kind, trusting to that day when we may meet again and grasp hands in friendship in our Father's kingdom where there shall be no further parting to endure.

You are not aware perhaps that I have recently established myself and my school in a new settlement. It is somewhat further up the same Saint Paul's River, but located in a very good place. I continue to make all the improvements I can, and I have quiet hopes for the future. I have now fourteen boys in school and two girls, all of whom are making some progress in reading the word of God. They are all native children, and I willingly labor amongst these little heathens, doing all I can according to your wishes. Last November I took a young American woman, a recent emigrant from Maryland, as my assistant and teacher. But alas she was soon sacrificed to the climate and called home to rest. I have every reason to believe that her journey was a peaceful one. Hers was the third death in the mission in a matter of weeks. We lost a boy with consumption, his malady lingering for a cruel length of time. The other unfortunate one died speedily, being seized with stomach pains at five in the morning, yet he caused such a commotion as to raise the whole village. By dawn he was no more, but his sad demise convinced a handful of our *scholars* to run off, for the native people among whom we live are still very superstitious. If someone dies suddenly, they are sure that somebody must have bewitched them, and off they will go to the grand devil man of the village who will, in exchange for some small trifle, tell them who it was that bewitched the person that died. This person will then be fed some poison in order to dispatch him for his wrongful deed. This appears to me not an entirely unjust method of administering justice, and one from which we of the so-called civilized world might learn something valuable.

Indeed, the natives are a much-maligned people in this dark and benighted country. Some of our less respectable emigrants find cause to torment and exploit these creatures, rather than try to fuse into their souls the values of American civilization with which their good masters labored to anoint them. In our neighboring settlement, a Mr Charles, an American, his money grown short due to the ruin of his smallholding near Monrovia, *borrowed* two native boys, informing their fathers that he was going to teach them English. Instead, he cruelly carried them to a slave factory and sold them for the equivalent of twelve dollars. In conversing with the natives, I often ask them how it is they cannot read and write like the white man (they call us all white man), and I generally receive reply that their gods had asked them to choose between the land and their livestock, or books, and they had chosen the former. At this juncture I often protest, and talk about the ingenious nature of native embroidery and craft, my contention being that our God has blessed the native with as much sense as any white man if only they would put this in exercise. The native is generally resigned to finally admitting that this *white man* does talk true, for I think they have become much fond of me.

Sadly, not all *masters* will converse in such a manner with these natives. Only last year, in an attack spurred on by revenge for native depredations upon settlers, the strongest and most populous native town on this part of the coast was taken, burned, and the natives powerfully routed, for they can be very savage when they think they have the advantage. At times like this, it is strange to think that these people of Africa are called our ancestors, for with some of them you may do all you can but they still will be your enemy. For many months now, there has been no sound of war amongst the neighboring tribes, and the affairs of the country appear quite smooth. We are all truly grateful that the war horn is heard no more, and the natives continue to display some friendship, for in this way we might avoid foolish loss of life. It was intended that Africa should be a land of freedom, for where else can the man of color enjoy his liberty? Not in Haiti or in Canada. This land of our forefathers, where many delicious fruits grow, is determined still to attract the noblest minds. If you hear any speaking disrespectful of it, I would be grateful if you would tell them to hush their mouths, for a lazy man, be he a gentleman or otherwise, will not prosper in any country should he determine that he will not work. Further, in this republic the practice is to address me as *Mr Williams* and not *Boy*. There are a few white people out here, and they are polite, moving to one side and touching their hats. In Monrovia, I have had occasion to call at their dwellings and to range over the subjects of the day, religious and otherwise. The white man never calls me by anything but my name. I am *Mr Williams*.

Sadly, I do not enjoy the same happy intercourse with the black emigrants hereabouts. Some emigrants, who styled themselves as lay ministers of the Gospel, asked permission to enter my new settlement and to preach the word of God. They gained admission with my blessing, and with that of the agents of the colony, as my present settlement lies beyond the furthest position in the interior to which we are generally encouraged to travel. However, our relationship soon soured as they took pleasure in forever recounting the number of hopeful converts who resided with them in their previous settlement, and how these converts were now filled with the Holy Ghost, their confidences awakened, and how they had become more friendly by the day. It was as though they made this continual assault upon my person in order to insult what they assumed to be the so-far modest achievements of my present mission. It appeared that amongst their biblical attachments were Methodist, Baptist and Presbyterian sentiments, and that so ill-schooled were they that clearly they could not distinguish one variety from the next, but I refrained from raising this subject. That they had truly embraced religion, that they displayed the patience to resist the temptations of the evil one, I did not doubt, but their criticism of my *dictatorial* manner and their suggestions on the moral value of my behavior proved too much, and, soon after their arrival, I ordered them to withdraw. They did so, but not before they had spread malicious gossip abroad that a child recently delivered to a native woman bore a strong and suspicious likeness to one Nash Williams. I countered, suggesting that this would appear only natural in that we shared the same ancestry, but in the minds of some emigrant farmers, a brace of whose number chose to leave my settlement, it appeared that the seeds of damage that these *ministers* had so wilfully scattered, were now finally beginning to bear some fruit.

Soon after the expulsion of my *ministers of the Gospel*, it became clear that I would have to look for one who was willing and able to help me in my labors amongst the heathen flock. To this end I travelled to Monrovia, where I engaged a young lady who was recently arrived from America, being formerly the property of a Mr Young of Pennsylvania. She informed me that she had come out to Africa last September, and had passed through her acclimatizing fevers very well. She seemed, to my eyes, ably prepared for the business of mission work, having been raised up in one of the best Christian families of America. The young lady returned with me up the Saint Paul's River, and although clearly a little disenchanted at first casting a glance over our small Christian empire, her eyes soon accustomed themselves to the more primitive conditions of the interior, so much so that she now acts and behaves as though she has known nothing else. I expect to be wedlocked to her in a short time, if life lasts and all things hold out. Perhaps you would be so kind as to send out something to start on in the way of making a living as a newly married couple, for you know that my time is not consumed in speculative affairs which are likely to result in my achieving worldly gains. The colony is not now as flourishing as it was, trade is dull, and the past season very unfavorable to the growth of all our main staffs of life.

As respects coffee, these days it sells at fifty cents per pound, but it grows wild and often natives and monkeys take it. Loaf sugar sells at twenty-eight dollars per hundred. Fresh beef will fetch twelve cents per pound. Cattle sell at fifteen dollars each, sheep two dollars, goats a dollar, hogs at different prices according to size from one dollar to fifteen, ducks at one dollar each, and fowls at two dollars per dozen. Laborers can be hired for twenty cents per day, and a person might have good common people to work the ground and make it as productive as that in America. But one word of explanation as to why such as I, who plant and work the land with application, still struggle, is to be found in the maxim that it is several years before farm land will pay. It has always been so, and so it will remain. There are some that have come to this place that have got rich, and done well, by using the natives as slaves. But invariably this means that the poor, unskilled people who come from America have no chance to make a living, for the natives do all the work. There is little chance for farming at Monrovia, for it is all stones. Out here, in the interior, there is good land, but unless one wishes to administer one's province in an uncharitable and cruel manner, the times are hard for all who would till the soil honestly.

Dear Father, perhaps you will please send me one bonnet and an umbrella, if you please. And some cloth to make one white frock, as there is none to be found in this country. These things will not prove difficult for you to get, for there is plenty in America and nothing here. Can you please send some valuable books, such as history, and a dictionary, and writing paper and quills or steel pens. Also flour and pork, and other articles you may think will be of service to me, including a hoe, an axe, some trowels and some hammers. If you, or any of your kind family to whom I am already under so many obligations, shall send anything for me, it shall not be misplaced charity, for provision is scarce.

I was very sorry to hear that my mother was dead, but I take great consolation in knowing that she has gone home to rest and we have nothing to do but to prepare to meet her. I am further consoled by your heartbroken intelligence that she died with Jesus in her soul and Heaven in her view, and her confidence well-anchored in the Lord. I have been in Africa a long time and I wish to come home as soon as possible. I wish you to write to me by the first emigrant vessel and let me know on what terms I can come back, and if I will be interrupted by white people. William Young left here shipped aboard a storeship, and I have heard from him twice. He is in Cincinnati acting as a porter in a merchant's store or warehouse, so it must be possible to successfully return. I would like very much to see you once in the flesh, and this may prove my last chance to cross the Atlantic. It is naturally my full intention to return to Liberia, for it is the best country for the black man that is to be found on the face of the earth. Older nations, with different styles of government, may be slow to acknowledge all that is due to us for whom the golden sun of liberty is newly rising. But Liberia is doing her part in improving human affairs, and stands now tall and proud with other regions of the civilized world.

Will you please be so kind as to let my friends know that I am well? I would inform them myself, but I am no longer sure of their circumstances. I think they would come over were they not afraid of the fever, but every person that comes to this country must naturally go through a course of sickness before they can expect to enjoy health. I wish you to be so kind as to remember my best respects to Lucy and Fanny Thornton, should you see them, and any enquiring friends. I intended to send some of all kinds of seeds on the first chance I have. I do not recollect of our losing anyone, besides those already mentioned, since you last had the pleasure of hearing from me, and all who know of you join with me in thanking you for your unspeakable kindness and goodness towards us which shall never be forgotten. It will not surprise you to learn that Mary Williams Lewis still distributes tracts on temperance, and remains an advocate for the cause of refraining from the use of ardent spirits. Those that take the pledge under her guidance are not known to take one more gill of spirit, for her doctrines are so-framed as to make the believer steadfast in the knowledge that he does this not only for himself, but for his country.

You must write to me by the first opportunity. I would send you some fruit, but the passage being expected to be long, I thought it would certainly spoil before it reached you. When I write again I will try to send some curiosities. You must excuse my bad writing as it is late. You give away no hints, but I really think some hard feelings against me on your part forms the reason I have received just one letter from you up until this present time. You know I will write to you as long as I can find a piece of paper. I beg to close by subscribing myself to be sincerely yours in the bonds of affection. I remain yours in love.

Nash Williams

Dear Father,

I trust that these few hasty lines which I set down with respect find you in good health and fine spirits. Why your heart remains hard against me is a mystery which has caused me emotions of great distress. But so it must be. I can never guide your hand. I was greatly disappointed on the arrival of the last emigrant vessel by not receiving a single line from you. You chose to comment, in your only letter to this date, that you still have affection. But why do I not receive letters more often? I am so situated that I cannot see every vessel that comes on the coast, but my name and settlement are broadly known in this region. I like this place very well, but my greatest desire is that I may see you once more in this world. I have followed your counsel as much as possible. You need not be afraid that I shall forget or neglect them.

Did I tell you of my partiality to a young woman hereabouts? After a short courtship I put my addresses to her, and I expect to be somewhat true to her till I die. We were married on the first of March, she being a native woman, and one of the best in Africa. She faithfully discharges the office of mother to a child I possess by another, less successful, connection, and she remains an industrious woman who performs all the duties relative to house-keeping, including making clothes for her *family*. This *family*, above whom I reign as head, join me in sending love to their good father whom they have never seen. My son, whom I have taken the liberty of naming Edward in the hope that he might emulate your esteemed self, will soon be in need of materials to help speed his skills in reading and writing. You will therefore send me something. Anything you may choose to send will be acceptable, and the sum of three hundred dollars, being of no consequence to a man of your wealth, would suffice. I would be very thankful for some newspapers, and if you wish I will send to you a few of ours. I hope, dear Father, that you will send me a few working tools such as axes and hoes, for the like are very useful, but very hard to get here.

The fever in these parts is not so bad now as it used to be, for it would seem that the older the place gets, and the more it is cultivated, the better the fever is. Having long passed through the acclimatizing process, and having watched others do so with equal success, I am glad that I can say that I love this country more than I did at first. The seasons here remain quite different from those in my old country, yet the weather seems to get cooler. This year we have been blessed with little rain, and the sun has parched up most of all of the crops in the fields, so if you would be so kind as to send me out something, I would feel much obliged. Anything, I do not mind what it is, for I feel sure that it will make a valuable contribution.

Farming is now our main occupation, the numbers at the mission school having fallen off in a dramatic manner. I have my fields planted with potatoes, arrowroot, cassava and considerable corn. In addition, I have a large number of cotton bushes, and a variety of other vegetables. I have also planted a large piece in rice, and together with the natives work from morning till sunset clearing and planting. I should be much obliged to you if you would send me a mill, for I have tried to cut a stone for that purpose, but found it beyond me. I am not in such a prosperous situation as might be expected, for it remains difficult to exchange produce for foreign produce, and besides, we make up just enough to sustain us from starvation. I have fowls in plenty, of all kinds. I have also hogs and goats. My horned cattle are only now beginning to increase, and some of the more skilled natives have, under my influence, made fences to secure them. They would, before this, often run out into the woods where they would quickly become lost. Keeping this rich land in order, and clean of grass and weeds, is my main task. But any man who will use common industry can raise much that he will eventually employ.

If, dear Father, these lines should find you in the land of the living, I will be more than glad to hear from you. I have written many letters to you at different times across the breadth of the last few years, and yet you seem reluctant to engage with me. I have come to the conclusion that you have repudiated me for reasons that perhaps owe their origins to some form of shame. Is there perhaps someone who has poisoned your mind against me? If these lines should find you in health, please return me an answer by the shortest way. My pleas with you to aid me, on behalf of all of this settlement, have been ill-received, for you have made nothing available to ease my present circumstances. Like all new countries, this is a very hard one, and some kindness on your part would have been pleasing to me. Should you have chosen to send me seeds of all description, I would have gladly made some use of them. I have given you full accounts of this place, so you can be in no doubt as to the often troubling nature of affairs hereabouts. That you have chosen to ignore my request that I might once more visit America to pay respects to my departed mother, and to cast my eyes upon old friends, has caused my heart to suffer in a great deal of pain. I have little opportunity for intercourse with familiar emigrants in these parts, for most of those who know of you are scattered all about the country, some few up here, but most down in the capital. So daily I wonder about those names across the water who, hearing no news, I constantly fear may have already departed this life.

Only last week I chanced to go into Monrovia in order that I might visit with old friends, both white and black. But not only could I not discern any news, it would appear that my present domestic arrangements have caused some offense to those who would hold on to America as a beacon of civilization, and an example of all that is to be admired. Are we not in Africa? This is what I constantly asked of the blacks. But it appeared they felt I merely sought to justify my *native* style of living. I counter-rallied and made it plain that I have nothing to justify, for amongst the emigrants I am indisputably the proudest holder of my race, but I soon found myself effectively shunned by my fellow Americans, many of whom privately mock African civilization whilst outwardly aping the fashion and posture of persons returned home. I realized that it would be beneficial for my health were I to cease conversation, withdraw, and return for ever to the safety of my Saint Paul's River settlement.

Sad to report, but before my retreat from the capital I was able to ascertain that these days the chief topic of conversation is that ancient immovable, slavery. Hardly a week passes on this coast of Africa without some report of a sea-bound slaver, and its unfortunate cargo, who have been afforded protection by the unfurling of the Star Spangled Banner. Without the hoisting of this emblem, the British man-of-wars would quickly, and happily, take these ships captive and liberate their black inhabitants. To most colored men, who reside here in liberty, and would expect liberty to encompass all of Africa, this dark land of our forefathers, this American protectionism is a disgrace to our dignity, and a stain on the name of our country. The hoisting of some other banner would be scarcely less insulting, but that they choose to sport our national flag, this is surely too much. But sadly, there is still more to be said on this subject of slavery. It appears that slave-dealers are establishing slave factories within the territory of Liberia, cunningly situating them further down the coast in the hope of avoiding prying eyes. The Governor recently ordered one such villain away, telling him he had no right to deal in slaves in that territory, and instructing him under threat of penalty that he must remove his factory in so many days. However, contrary to his agreement, he would not do so, and so the factory was broken up and forty puncheons of rum turned loose on the ground. There are those in Monrovia who profit handsomely from this *business*, and who would choose to ignore the existence of such evil deeds and their correction, but the problems of slavery continue to plague us, yes, even here in the bosom of liberty.

The rains are still with us, and the sky continues to open its heart and shed tears upon all the known earth. Master, you took me into your house as a young boy and instructed me in the ways of civilized man. Under your tutelage, I acquired whatever rude skills I now possess in the art of reading and writing, and more besides. Why have you forsaken me? There are many things I cannot discuss with my native wife, for it would be improper for her to share with me the memories of what I was before. I am to her what she found here in Africa. If this is to be goodbye, then let it be with love and respect in equal portion. I must close these hasty lines by saying I remain your affectionate son.

Nash Williams

Just when Edward's recovery appeared complete, he was seized again by another severe fever and the accompanying shivering. He dragged his wretched body back to the safety of his bed, and, as the British doctor applied a cold towel to his head, he closed his bloodshot eyes. Sadly, Edward's stubborn fever refused to break, and merciful sleep eluded him as his mind ranged back and forth. When sleep did come it was soon destroyed by demons which prodded at his memory as though it were an open wound. Accordingly, at night he chose instead to lie perfectly still, the towel now hot and burning his brow, his stubbled aspect irritating him to the point of madness, and he simply stared out of the window and up into the black African sky. The thick heat of this devil's climate clung to him like a woven blanket, and he was constantly visited by that unwelcome guest, thirst. Edward prayed earnestly, and with devotion, that he might be spared these days and nights of sad affliction, and that his health be soon restored to him.

Some two weeks later, his gait betraying little of his recent bout of illness, Edward was once more able to walk about unaided. The doctor informed him that he was now acclimatized, and whilst he must continue to be ever vigilant with regard to the many diseases which abounded on the African coast, his worst fears were over. Edward secured temporary lodgings down by the harbor, and then set about making enquiries as to how he might obtain a passage to Liberia. A Dutch sea captain, who chanced to be drinking in the same tavern as Edward, informed him that whilst he was battling with the fever, whatever dispute it was that had occasioned the cessation of civilities between Sierra Leone and Liberia had been successfully concluded. Apparently, he would simply have to await the arrival of a ship that would agree to transport him. Edward thanked the gentleman, and listened as the sad, drawn-out sound of a bugle being blown from the parapets of the British fortress signalled the end of the day. As the last note drifted away and across the sea, Edward emptied his tankard, gathered up his cane, tipped his hat, and retired to his rented rooms, where he slept and dreamed soundly, and passed a blessed night without once breaking sweat.

The following afternoon, Edward engaged the services of the first mate of an American trading vessel. The experienced *sea dog* advised Edward that they would be setting sail on the evening tide, which meant there would be little time for Edward to occupy himself with spiritual preparation for the journey ahead. He simply hurried back to his rooms, gathered his belongings, paid the landlord, and employed a sturdy native to convey his boxed personal effects to the ship. The moon shimmered on the wrinkled face of the sea, and a stern breeze bellied out the sail. Edward settled in, and decided that he would pass most of his time sitting out on deck amongst the bales of luggage, breathing deeply of the salty air, and staring at the gleaming shoals of flying fish which leapt to either side of the ship. His inner being was filled with a strange tranquillity, and a deep peace fell upon him at least the equal to any he had ever known in his life, although the origins and purpose of this strangely contemplative mood eluded him. In his mind he would rehearse scenes from the life of Christ, yet found that even in Christ's moments of greatest adversity, such as when betrayed by Judas, or when being led to the Cross, his Lord's face never lost its purity and compassion. Edward wondered if this peace were not perhaps the heralding of his impending demise, but when this thought fought its way into his mind, he redoubled his strength and immediately banished it.

There was simply no way of Edward discovering whether the man with whom he most eagerly desired an audience, namely Madison Williams, had received the letter informing him of Edward's intention to set sail for Liberia, and giving him notice of the anticipated week of arrival. Following the souring of Edward's relationship with this difficult man, when it became clear to all that a junior slave, Nash, had supplanted Madison in the master's affections, Madison, a strong, proud man, both of character and stature, had withdrawn from the house and, in the privacy of the slave village, intensified his efforts to acquaint himself with the Bible and with the skills of reading and writing. After nearly two years, in which Madison rejected Edward's many overtures towards him, perhaps recognizing that they originated in Edward's guilt at having surrendered to his own changing passions, a sober-looking Madison had presented himself at the house and requested an audience of his master. When Edward appeared he announced that he now considered himself sufficiently educated, and properly acquainted with God's ways, to have earned his freedom and subsequent transportation to the new African territory of Liberia. Edward, who had long desired the opportunity of bestowing upon Madison a gesture of good-will, hurriedly agreed to Madison's request and asked if there were anything further that he might do. Madison shook his head firmly, bowed and withdrew. Soon after, he made his preparations to depart for Africa. His subsequent letters to Edward, though brief, had remained polite. Through them, Edward was able to discover that Madison had settled in Monrovia and was eking out a living as a small trader selling palm oil, rice, camwood and animal skins to passing European and American ships. As this short voyage unfolded, Edward arrived at the uncomfortable conclusion that, perhaps because of the warmth of their first encounters, or perhaps this and the additional fact that the passage of time had served to sever Edward's links with many of his other former charges, Madison had now become the only person in Africa whom he felt he could trust. Indeed, it had been to Madison that he had immediately turned when faced with the unpleasant details of Nash's abrupt and final message. He would now have little choice but to place his entire confidence in this man.

Edward's first sighting of Monrovia came at dawn, but it certainly did not occasion his heart to leap with joy. In fact, Edward felt himself suddenly overcome with an ill-feeling of foreboding. The morning sea was beautiful and calm, and held in her embrace a number of small offshore islands. Beyond these rushed the boiling surf, where the low waves bit at the shore and foamed white, but thereafter was misery. Edward stared at the gathering of low, square huts, seemingly built of sticks and mud, walls leaning drunkenly to the north or south of vertical, clumsily thatched and adorned with grass, or a flattering crown of corrugated iron. Behind these dwellings he could see only a forested horizon which appeared to mask a huge, roaming jungle in which nothing stirred, and whose only sound was a mournful roar of silence. As Edward clutched the rail and watched, it would have been impossible for any onlooker to have guessed to what depths of loneliness he had now sunk. He looked up into the sky and saw rain clouds beginning to form and flow through the sky like huge ships, although by now he had come to understand that, in this zone, rain was little more than a precursor of the heat to follow. Back on land there was neither a whisper, nor a sign of movement from the ragged cluster of abodes which lined the shore. A despondent Edward leaned forward and set his face towards the bottomless ocean.

Within the hour the ship had anchored off the African port of Monrovia, and the passengers and freight were being gingerly reunited with *terra firma* by means of a fleet of small launches. As his ill-made craft picked its leaky way through the surf, Edward noticed the fishing boats, their nets suspended from tall poles and drying in the sun before being once more thrown to the deep, and he reached the conclusion that these vessels of commerce seemed far better equipped for sea-faring than his present mode of transportation. Fortunately, the low wind merely ruffled the surface of the ocean, otherwise he was sure that both he and his boxes would have succumbed to a watery end. Once on shore, Edward clasped a handkerchief to his mouth and nose to ward off the fetid African air, but the sudden mist of mosquitoes could be combatted only by his swatting them against his skin, until his forearm was decorated with a series of red blotches. Suddenly, natives and colored Americans were everywhere, anxious to greet the arrival of this new ship, and in their wake they created a veritable din. Edward examined them, particularly the natives, their semi-clad bodies ensnared by large corded muscles, but amongst their numbers he was unable to recognize any who had about them a demeanor which suggested that they might have been sent by Madison to greet him. And then the weather, being predictable in this region only in its excesses, suddenly, and without warning, changed, and the rain teemed from the skies. At moments such as this it was customary for a Christian gentleman to acknowledge that such a downpour, whilst causing inconvenience to the human being, inevitably bestowed much satisfaction and benediction upon God's shrubbery, his crops, and his trees. However, the sudden outburst served only to irritate Edward and, following the example of others about him, he abandoned his boxes and marched with some purpose towards the shelter of an overhanging palm tree, whose branches hung limply as though they had been exhausted by the heat of many days. Edward examined the stout gray trunk, and fingered the grainy ridges which ascended as though a series of healed wounds. The rain began now to increase in volume, and Edward realized that he was effectively marooned until the wind chose to rise and blow the clouds to some other part of Africa.

When the rain ceased, Edward entrusted his belongings to a

colored American boy, whom he guessed to be not in excess of
twenty years, and whom he observed to be a decent specimen.
The boy asked of his *master* in which direction they were
headed. Edward, who still carried within his bosom some idle
hope that he might recognize a former slave from among the
throng at the dockside, now found himself in the lamentable
position of having to ask advice from his employee. Under
questioning, it appeared that this boy was aware of decent
lodgings where white people could comfortably accommodate
themselves. Edward had presumed that such places would be
difficult to locate, for the idea was that Liberia would be
established as the country of the free blacks, and Edward had
imagined that those white men who dared the seas to arrive
in Liberia would have little choice but to join with the more
civilized negroes in the sharing of all manner of facilities, even
those most basic to mankind. He had further presumed that
this policy would no doubt prevent some *opinionated* white
men, both traders and seamen alike, from tarrying too long
in Liberia, if they chose to visit at all, but it had been argued,
by those of a liberal disposition, that perhaps these were not
the quality of men that this new country wished to attract.
However, Edward's employee assured him that lodgings for
white gentlemen were indeed available.

The young colored boy, his person severely burdened by
Edward's effects, led his *master* through the unkempt and
overgrown streets of Monrovia. Edward could not help but
notice what appeared to him to be appalling conditions, and
he kept his handkerchief pressed close to nose and mouth
against the truly foul smell which cleaved the air. Others,
however, both white and colored, appeared unconcerned by
this atmosphere, which led Edward to speculate as to whether
or not he might, in the fullness of time, become similarly
familiar with the unwholesome character of this Africa. The
boarding house to which the bondsman led Edward bore
some similarities to the one in Sierra Leone where he had
recently dwelt. A wooden, two-storey affair, a thin coat of

white paint and a small veranda bestowed upon this simple building an air of majesty. The colored boy stopped and lay down his boxes, as though unsure of his choice, but with a friendly nod of his head Edward made it clear to the boy that these premises were acceptable.

The room was sparsely furnished, but with good taste. Edward eyed the mosquito net, which draped itself purposefully about the bed, and imagined that this would no doubt prove the most important item in the room. The window gave out on to a small courtyard where the clamor of commerce might, according to the black innkeeper, prove a trifle deafening in the daytime, but come the evening there would be neither sound nor song to disturb the slumber of his new guest. The man withdrew and left Edward together with the boy. It was at this juncture that Edward thought it politic to ask after the young man whether or not he was in possession of either a wife or a girl. To this the boy smiled shyly, then shook his head. Edward examined the young man, his perfect shape, strong torso, powerful legs, and then sat down on one corner of the bed. The bondsman remained standing, although he moved uneasily from one foot to the next as though unsure what was expected of him. And then Edward, sensing the young man's discomfort, simply leaned forward and asked after his name. The boy averted his eyes, and, keeping the screen of his lashes low, he whispered the single word 'Charles.' 'I see,' replied Edward, rising to his feet. 'Charles, I will be taking a short rest. Perhaps you might try to locate for me the whereabouts of one Madison Williams, a former slave on my plantation and now, according to his testimony, residing hereabouts.' At this juncture, Edward produced a piece of paper and held it out. However, before Charles could take it into his grasp, Edward withdrew the paper and made proper enquiry as to whether the young man could read. On receiving assurance that he could, Edward once more proffered the paper, which Charles took into his hand. 'Once you have located Madison Williams, you will inform him that I desire to hold an audience with him at his earliest convenience, is this clear?' Charles nodded his head and bowed silently. Then, without taking his eyes from his employer, he backed out of the room and gently closed in the door behind him.

Some hours later, Edward heard a light knocking upon his door, and he jumped from the bed, startled by this unadvertised interruption to his slumber. Realizing that it must be Charles returning with news of Madison, he called to the black retainer, ordering him not to stray from his present position. Edward pulled about himself a loose gown, and then gently cracked the door and ushered in a sheepish-looking Charles. Edward thought it best to say little, and to give the chance to the young man, which proved to be the correct decision. No sooner had the door been pushed to behind him, and Edward guided him into a chair, than Charles immediately set forth on his tale of disappointment. Apparently he had, with little difficulty, located the house of Madison Williams, but when he arrived there he discovered the abode to be in a state of abandonment. It was not that it was either broken-down or weather-beaten in its appearance, but merely that it looked as though whosoever had formerly occupied the premises had departed in some haste. By standing on the tips of his toes and staring through the window, Charles was able to see that everything had been left in a state of disarray. It was at this moment that Charles was apprehended by a well-dressed man, in the company of his lady wife, who, pointing an umbrella in the direction of the younger and less worldly man, demanded of him an explanation as to his behavior. Charles had stammered a little before blurting out the information that he had been sent by his *master* to convey a message to one Madison Williams. On hearing this, the well-dressed man let it be known that Madison Williams had indeed left suddenly, to go up-river to attend to some business, the full nature of which the gentleman was unsure about. He was polite with his information, and further explained that he imagined that his friend, Madison, would be returning to Monrovia in the next day or two, for it was unknown that he should be absent from *home* for any protracted period of time. Edward listened carefully to all that the animated Charles related, his eyes never leaving the young man's face. At the conclusion of the tale, Edward stood, reached into his pocket and pressed a coin upon Charles, who in turn muttered his thanks and made ready to take his leave. Edward informed young Charles that he expected him to visit at Madison's house three times each day, morning, noon and evening, until the fellow returned. When he did so, Charles was to inform him immediately that his former master requested an audience with him as soon as possible. In the mean time, should Charles want for anything, he was to make it his business to appear at Edward's lodgings, at any suitable hour, and reveal to Edward, without fear or embarrassment, the full nature of his needs. At this, Charles expressed gratitude, promised to do as instructed, and retired from the room.

The evening was suddenly upon him. An overheated Edward, sweat sliding from his armpits and down his sides, examined his ashen flesh, observing with some distaste his stomach, where the skin was wrinkled like paint. After the departure of Charles, he had once more fallen asleep, but this time he had choked on a succession of unpleasant dreams and awoken in a fury, the sheet knotted about him as though he had fought with the bed in his sleep. Certain that further sleep would elude him for some hours yet, he dressed quickly, pausing only to inspect his ageing body and to listen as a rat ran across the thin boards of the ceiling. Then, satisfied that he was attired in a proper manner, he stepped out into the streets in search of some innocent amusement. In this Africa it appeared that both dawn and dusk were brief and ambiguous, as though there were little time to waste, and Edward soon found himself enveloped in gloom. In the distance, he heard the quiet engine of the sea continually renewing itself, and echoing across the night. Then he momentarily stiffened with fear as a dog whose sick-eye ran with water stepped casually out of the darkness. The ribbed mongrel hobbled awkwardly and eyed Edward in the hope of some morsel of food, but Edward glared back and thought about tossing a stick, for he considered it undignified to beg, and for this reason he found dogs repellent.

Pausing at the first tavern, Edward glanced through the open door and was pleased to discover the place mercifully free of clientele. He entered, removed his hat, and sat at the nearest table. He signalled to the boy with his cane, and he came quickly to him, over-delighted in a childish manner to see custom in the form of a white gentleman. Edward made his demands known and settled back to cast his mind forwards and backwards across this problem of his former slave, Nash. That he had banished not only Nash, but many of his other slaves, to this inhospitable and heathen corner of the world disturbed Edward. The boy arrived and delivered a foaming tankard of beer to Edward's table, and Edward rewarded him with a generous coin. The buffoon smiled and capered into the corner, and Edward supped carefully at the beer, his elbow bending like a stubborn hinge. Perhaps, thought Edward, this business of encouraging men to engage with a past and a history that are truly not their own is, after all, ill-judged. The light in the candle flickered, shadows danced against the white stone wall, and Edward drew again on his beer. It occurred to him that perhaps the fever, the sleepless nights, the complex welter of emotions that he had been subjected to since his arrival in Africa, were nothing more complex than manifestations of a profound guilt.

In a vain effort to banish the despair of this moment, and hopefully ensure a peaceful night's sleep free of demons, Edward raised his hand and once more summoned the boy to him. An hour or so later, his person much refreshed by consumption, and risking offense by leaving a tankard unfinished, Edward struggled out and picked his way down to the harbor. Once there, he gazed upon the tranquil sea, the moonlight sparkling on the water so that it looked like a liquid case of jewels. And then his attention was seized by the echoing of heels upon flaggings, and the loud protestations of a woman who declaimed lunatic phrases as though speaking some foolish part she had written for herself. Judging her an Irish whore by dint of her accent, Edward stared at her as she trembled in her cloud of wounded indignation, the thick powder on her face channeled with tears, her mouth set in a twist, and he felt pity and despair in equal part.

The following morning the braying of the traders and the incessant barking of dogs roused Edward from a troubling sleep. He fetched a deep sigh and cast a glance towards the small window, through which he could see that the clear, unclouded blue of the sky promised a murderously hot day, at least the equal of those he had already endured. He turned in the bed, careful not to disturb the mosquito netting, and realized that last night he had forgotten to pinch out the candle. A lump of misshapen wax overflowed the shallow dish. Then, a series of stifled coughs rattling through his body, Edward stepped urgently from the bed and first poured and then drank a glass of water. Perching on the edge of a chair, he soothed his dry throat with a further glass, and wondered if the boy Charles had left any message for him. Abandoning his desire for more slumber, he dressed quickly and sought out the innkeeper in order that he might make enquiry of Charles. Having located his host, he was informed by him that there was neither message, nor had there been any visit by Charles or any other, which caused Edward momentarily to panic and wonder whether the black bondsman had for some reason chosen to abandon him. Choosing not to dwell upon this unpleasant thought, Edward enquired after a club in which he might discover the company of white men and share with them some words, reasoning that if he was to be expected to pass yet more time in this savage environment, then he ought at least to be exposed to some of the pleasantries which civilized company can bestow upon a man's otherwise wretched African existence. The negro innkeeper, his face suddenly closed and his eyes lowered, informed Edward that he knew of a colonial club whose members were, as he termed them, *masters*.

Armed with directions to this place, which lay not too far off, Edward set forth across the town, the sun hanging above him like a bright lamp. He could feel small beads of sweat forming on his forehead and trickling down his temples, and others sliding about the bridge of his nose and then down and under his chin to his collar. He pulled out a handkerchief and dabbed furiously at his face as he walked. Having located the door to the club, Edward raised the brass knocker and struck it three times with force. A black man, clearly of American origin, answered and asked after his business, to which Edward answered that he had been given to believe that this was a Gentleman's Club for white people. As a visitor, he simply craved some companionship and some information as to how things went in these parts. Edward was surprised to discover the degree of hostility that this experience occasioned in his soul. Never before had he had to explain or ask anything of a colored man, and to have to do so now, and in order to gain access to the company of other white men, he found extremely difficult. The colored man listened carefully and then announced that he would soon return, a reply calculated to check, not encourage, enquiry. He closed in the door and left Edward standing in the street like a beggar.

Some moments later, the door was opened by the same fellow, and Edward was ushered into the comfortable and well-appointed vestibule of the brick house. Only when he surveyed the prints, and other wall décor, did it become apparent that this must be the abode of one of the principals of the American Colonization Society. Edward followed the servant into a drawing-room that was cluttered with books and papers, and well-finished with couches and loungers. Three white men, their skins grown dark through familiarity with the sun, rose as he entered, and hands were proffered and enquiries made. The already uncorked wine was poured into a glass, which was then thrust into Edward's willing hand. Thereafter followed an engrossing session, in which a cautious Edward shared his circumstances with those that came and went, and sought from them similar stories all relating to the common question of how it was they had come to find themselves adrift and washed up on this furthest shore of civilization. Anecdotes and faint memories were traded, and some attempts were made to swell them into order with dates and places. Edward stayed for lunch, then coffee, but thought it wise to retire before dinner, for by now he was fearful that news of the personal tragedy that had recently enveloped his name might somehow have crossed the waters and reached the ears of these gentlemen. He reasoned that before the confessional urge took hold of any tongue, he should request his cane. Edward stood, thanked them most warmly for a splendid day, and made ready to return to his lodgings.

Slightly merry on account of the good wine, a contented Edward asked the innkeeper after Charles, only to be informed that up until this very moment there had been no sign of the young bondsman. Edward returned to his hot and airless room with a bottle of claret, his mood rudely transformed by this news. Slipping into an involuntary sleep, he found his mind populated with images of Amelia, her face decorated with pond-like sores where flies and other creatures drank greedily. As dawn began to break over Monrovia, Edward awoke in a sweat and thrashed the covers off himself. Tears misted his eyes, for indeed his love for Amelia had festered and become stamped with a self-pity that was near-cousin to self-loathing. He simply craved to be offered the unconditional love of a child, could she not understand this? He looked ashamedly at the mauve contusions that decorated the several folds of his skin, and realized that the years had descended and smothered him like a fog. What else now but to submit to the indifferent squalor of old age, and give himself up to his fears? Edward let his feet fall over the side of the bed and brush the wooden floor, then he decided that if Charles did not show himself by the end of the day, he would go in person to Madison Williams's home and make enquiry. In the interim, he would do the next best thing, which was to spend another day in the company of his civilized countrymen.

As Edward dressed, his mind turned back again upon Amelia. Clearly she would have hated this Africa that Edward now felt marooned in. It had struck him, while at the club, that the lack of civilized white women in these parts would only have served to drive home her suspicion of all things African. Not only would curious, perhaps desparate, white eyes have travelled the length of her body, but black eyes would no doubt have made her the object of much unwanted attention. Edward ceased his wardrobe, fell to his knees, and prayed to the Lord that he might be forgiven for his indifference towards Amelia, for in truth no harm or misery had been intended. That she took it upon herself to sabotage her husband's friendship with Nash by destroying the colored man's letters was a painful discovery for Edward, but had he not found it in his heart to forgive her? Her accusation that in the wake of Nash's departure he was now making a fool of himself by lavishing an excess of affection upon a new retainer, was this not again met with forgiveness? That she had subsequently chosen to flee his home, then her mind, then this mortal world at the instigation of her own hand, was a tragedy the responsibility for which could not reside at Edward's doorstep. Surely his dear father understood this? A half-dressed Edward reached for his Bible, and clumsily fingered the pages until he reached the relevant verse. Thereafter, his wretched body burning with faith, he began to recite aloud.

Late in the morning, having left instructions with the inn-keeper that he should, at all costs, delay Charles if he chanced to arrive during Edward's absence, a somewhat despondent Edward stepped out into the street and followed much the same route as the previous day. When he arrived at the club, Edward seized the brass knocker and rapped three times, and the same colored man soon appeared before him. Only this time the man informed Edward that the members, having last night convened an extraordinary meeting which lasted into the small hours, had decided that Edward was not welcome, either as a visitor or as a member, should he choose to linger on these shores. Edward stared at the liveried servant and asked if he might be blessed with a reason, but the colored man, clutching self-righteously at his lapels as though they were a badge of some importance, simply eyed him with the manner of one who is happily charged only to deliver decisions and not to share with the unfortunate recipient the highways and byways that were explored in order to reach the proffered conclusion. Edward tarried a moment, scratched the skin under one eye, then, realizing that he was making little headway, turned on his heels, anxious that he should avoid having to suffer the ignominy of the door being slammed in his face.

Edward reached the inn, his mind in a daze, and discovered Charles standing with a travel-weary but finely dressed man whom he instantly recognized as Madison Williams. Immediately, Edward's gloom abated, and he shook hands firmly with his former slave, who, by all appearances, appeared to be well suited to the life of a free man. Edward dismissed Charles with a proffered coin, but the young man looked a little forlorn and asked if there might be some other way in which he could be of service to the *master*. Clearly Edward's curt dismissal had stung the young man like a lash, and the hurt that was now painted across his boyish face begged the older man to be kinder to him. Edward relented, and told him that he could, if he so wished, return tomorrow, and with this news a somewhat chastened Charles smiled, nodded cheerfully, and took his leave. Anxious not to waste any more time, Edward ordered the innkeeper to prepare food and wine for Madison and himself, which they would take in due course. With this request made, they retreated into Edward's room, and Edward signalled that Madison should make himself at ease in the more comfortable of the two chairs.

As Madison sat opposite him, Edward could not help but note that his former slave's person became suddenly very grave, the flesh frowning on his brow. Madison leaned forward. He spoke slowly and carefully, as though anxious that he should not be misunderstood. 'Master, Nash Williams is dead.' Edward recoiled slightly, as though he had been struck. 'The fever called him home. And he is burned according to local custom. This much I found out in the place from where I am happily returning.' A long silence deepened. Edward stared back at Madison and made no attempt to dam the tears which now flowed down his face. Eventually Madison stood. At this signal, Edward drew a hand across his cheeks. 'I shall return,' announced Madison, 'with more news.' Without waiting for further instruction, Madison withdrew and closed in the door behind him. Some moments later, the innkeeper knocked at the door with the requested food and drink, but Edward simply called for him to take it away and sank further into his grief. Nash Williams, the boy he had brought from the fields to the house, the boy who won his love, freely given, who would force on to him all the pain and confusion which finally proved too much for Amelia to bear, this Nash Williams was no more? And he, Edward, having travelled half the known world once again to be with him, what was he to do?

Edward spent the remainder of the day, and the full length of the night, sitting upright in the chair, his anguished mind questing in every conceivable direction, but forever stumbling into blind alleyways which proved to be swept clean of any meaning. In the morning Madison returned and found his former master in the same position in which he had left him, though Madison observed, by virtue of Edward's vacant stare, that there had been a considerable decline in his mental state.

He sat opposite Edward, but his former master gazed back at him as though he were not there. Madison spoke quietly and at length about Nash's final country settlement, and about the many problems which Nash had to face by choosing to live among the natives, but Edward remained silent. For some time, they simply stared at each other, each one a prisoner of their innermost thoughts. And then Madison reached into his pocket and pulled clear a letter. He informed Edward that this letter had been placed into his hands by Nash on the understanding that Madison would personally give it to his former master, and to him alone, even though it was understood that this would mean crossing the sea and returning to America. Edward looked more intently now. 'Did Nash not know I was coming?' Madison narrowed his eyes. 'You chose not to write to him.' Madison paused. 'And by the time I discovered him he was merely a few hours this side of death.' Edward dropped his gaze. Then he whispered, 'I want to go to where Nash lived.' Madison bestowed a scornful glare upon his former master. 'I have to go there.' Madison said nothing. He held out the letter. 'It is for you.' He paused. 'I promised Nash that I would deliver it to you personally.' Edward took the letter and looked at the envelope. He squeezed it gently. 'I have to go to where Nash lived.' Madison climbed to his feet.

Dear Father,

Despite my earlier protestations, I resort again to pen and paper in a final attempt to engage with you. I find the process humiliating, and I fail to see what hurt I ever inflicted upon you that could justify such a cruel abandonment of your past intimate, namely myself. There is much to report, but being unsure of how it might interest you, if at all, it is my intent to be brief.

My three wives (I have considered a fourth, but the expense is at present beyond me) are faring well, as are the children. Six in total, all of whom receive lengthy instruction in reading and writing which sits well upon their shoulders. In addition they receive, from their mothers, instruction in the African language, as I do. I feel the necessity of being able to understand properly the words of the natives in whose land I reside, and the inconvenience, self-denial and hardship I suffer on this count is clearly worth-while if it facilitates my being able freely to communicate with those hereabouts. That children learn faster, and with less inhibition than their elders and betters, is daily proven as we sit together and try to drink up these strange words and sounds. That my present family does not conform to what you might reasonably expect of me will no doubt disturb you. However, despite their heathen origins, my wives send their best respects to you, but nothing further, for you would scorn their poor marks were they to attempt written words. They had no school to attend, and have suffered accordingly, but not in their generosity of heart, or in their ability to act out the role of dear and gentle mother to their precious children. They know also how to administer to the needs of a husband, for as I chanced to mention in an earlier communication, the climate of this country does not suit old sores. Two such *fellows* have long since taken up residence on my left leg, and although I am obliged to suffer a little for want of a cure, my wives seek all the while to ease my discomfort with as much care and attention that I might reasonably expect from an American-born woman. Some months ago, I was quite afflicted by the death of my youngest child, a fine boy of about nine months. A large and healthy child, he was taken ill quite suddenly, and died thereafter. I am not able to say what his sickness was, for this remains a mystery even to those closest to him, who continue to grieve.

Perhaps you imagine that this Liberia has corrupted my person, transforming me from the good Christian colored *gentleman* who left your home, into this heathen whom you barely recognize. But this is not so, for, as I have often stated many times over, Liberia is the finest country for the colored man, for here he may live by the sweat of his brow, although everything remains scarce and high, such as provisions, clothing, etc. There are still many out here, and more arriving with each ship, who are not prepared for freedom, and who get on poorly because there is no one to act for them, and they are totally incapable of acting for themselves. But this is not the fault of the country, for although not free from famine, war, sickness and death, and other troubles incidental to mankind, I still proclaim that it will compare favorably with any other part of the habitable world. Persons coming to Africa, white or colored, should always remember that this is a new country and that everything has still to be created. Things can be both inconvenient and uphill, and many hardships will no doubt be experienced, but such problems are common to the first settlement in any country. We, the colored man, have been oppressed long enough. We need to contend for our rights, stand our ground, and feel the love of liberty that can never be found in your America. Far from corrupting my soul, this Commonwealth of Liberia has provided me with the opportunity to open up my eyes and cast off the garb of ignorance which has encompassed me all too securely the whole course of my life.

These days I am happy simply to raise my crops. The land is rich and produces the familiar American garden stuff, cabbage, peas, beans, onions, tomatoes, etc., as well as the native produce, which it does in abundance. The school is no more, and shall never again occupy a position of authority in any settlement of which I am a part. This missionary work, this process of persuasion, is futile amongst these people, for they never truly pray to the Christian God, they merely pray to their own gods in Christian guise, for the American God does not even resemble them in that most fundamental of features. The truth is, our religion, in its purest and least diluted form, can never take root in this country. Its young shoots will wither and die, leaving the sensible man with the conclusive evidence that he must reap what grows naturally. It has taken my dark mind many years to absorb this knowledge, and while it would be true to assert that the man I love is Christ, and I love him as one might love an intimate, having no means to return to America, and being therefore bound to an African existence, I must suspend my faith and I therefore freely choose to live the life of the African.

If it please you, I wish you to remember me kindly to my colored friends. Inform them that should they choose to come out to this country, then they must bring everything for housekeeping, farming and carpentry, etc. They will need them, for they cannot be got here nor, unless their master chooses to be bonded to his promises, can they be obtained by means of purchase from the packet. It only remains that I request of you that you do not come out to Africa, for I fear I will surely disappoint you. I suppose I shall never again see you in this life, but if the Lord so deems it, I might yet cast my eyes upon you on the pleasant banks of deliverance. Perhaps in this realm of the hereafter you might explain to me why you used me for your purposes and then expelled me to this Liberian paradise. I believed fiercely in all that you related to me, and fervently hoped that one day I might be worthy of the name I bore, the learning I had been blessed with, and the kind attentions of a master with the teachings of the Lord fused into his soul. That my faith in you is broken, is evident. You, my father, did sow the seed, and it sprouted forth with vigor, but for many years now there has been nobody to tend to it, and being abandoned it has withered away and died. Your work is complete. It only remains for me once more to urge you to remain in your country.

Nash Williams

Madison Williams appeared at the rooming house and enquired of the innkeeper as to the general well-being of his former master. The innkeeper slowly shook his head, and informed Madison that for three days now he had neither seen nor heard from the gentleman. Sadly, he presumed his guest to be still in a state of distress. Madison thanked him for his intelligence and, acting upon the innkeeper's suggestion, he made his way to Edward's room. He knocked, but there was no answer, so he knocked again, this time more briskly. From inside he heard a muted cry to enter. Madison opened the door and, peering through a gloom that belonged to neither night nor day, he discovered Edward prostrate upon the bed, and Nash's letter scattered about the floor.

The room had a heavy, musty smell, the drapes having been pulled against the world for three whole days. Edward, as though suddenly conscious of his lamentable appearance, heaved himself into an upright position, rubbed a hand into his face, and then, with some difficulty, stood and made some efforts to stretch. Madison remained standing by the door, unsure as to whether or not he wished to witness this spectacle. Then, through a small chink in the drapes, a slither of light hit Edward and, taking this as a signal, he drew back the coarse material and flooded the room. Madison lifted his arm to his face and awaited his cue, but for the moment at least Edward chose to remain silent. He carefully positioned himself at the foot of the bed and, as he pulled on his leather shoes and strapped them into place, he observed Madison out of the corner of his eye. Madison chose to ignore him, and instead looked all about himself, studying the sparsely furnished room. There was something about the small room, the many hours of darkness having cooled the air and created a welcome respite from the familiar heat, which suggested to Madison that whatever business had to be carried on in these parts had been concluded. Madison knew, without his former master saying anything, that Edward was ready to leave. He expected an announcement.

Edward cleared his throat and spoke slowly, but forcefully. 'I wish,' he began, 'to be taken immediately to where Nash Williams conducted his affairs.' Madison looked hard at Edward. Detecting Madison's opposition, Edward repeated himself. 'I wish you to conduct me to the Nash Williams settlement.' Madison nodded once, careful to make his nod an acknowledgement of his understanding the words, and not an agreement to act upon them. 'Well?' asked a suddenly animated Edward. 'When do we leave?' 'Perhaps in a day or two,' suggested Madison. 'How long do you wish to tarry there?' Edward snorted in disbelief, and then laughed out loud. 'A day or two! We leave today. And I will tarry there as long as I desire.' Madison adjusted his posture, and then explained to Edward that should they leave immediately they would inevitably have to spend this coming evening in a settlement between the capital and Nash's own former place of residence, for the distance was simply too great to be covered in what remained of this day. A river canoe would have to be engaged, and a navigator found. Supplies would have to be purchased. Precautions taken. Madison listed off the various stages of preparation that still needed to be passed through, but even as he spoke he could see that nothing was going to deflect the smiling Edward from his chosen course. The man's mind was fevered with determination.

The river wore a rutted frown where their slow progress had disturbed her sleep. To either side the somber banks, cluttered

with trees, shrubs and vines, were pressed by a thick, brooding
undergrowth that was heavy with years. As dusk approached,
the heat still hung low like a ceiling above their heads. Madison
uttered some words in the local language and the native
helmsman, a reed of a man who could clearly boast no associa-
tion with books, and whose liquor-stained breath announced
his common mode of recreational activity, began to paddle
towards the northern shore. The mosquitoes redoubled their
attentions, and Edward crushed another against his blotched
arm and asked if this place was to mark their journey's end
for this day. As the canoe neatly avoided the clean stones, and
fetched up on a muddy shelf, Madison replied that he knew of
a settlement hereabouts where, according to his calculations,
they should receive a peaceful welcome. However, he advised
Edward that perhaps he ought not to mention the true purpose
which lay behind their visit, for there were those who would
not consider a pilgrimage to the site of Nash Williams's demise
an honorable journey.

Madison followed a stamped-in path through the tall grass,
and Edward, ignoring the irritating bite of a nail in his boot,
and the native tracked close behind. A little more than one
hundred paces from the river bank, Madison stopped suddenly
and pointed through the bush towards a village. Tall brown
huts were huddled together within a clumsy fence, and a
faint wind lifted human voices and stirred Edward's curiosity.
Choosing not to speak, Madison edged forward through the
drooping foliage and into the heart of this village which,
much to Edward's consternation, was soon revealed to be,
not a native settlement, but one populated by Americans
who spoke English. The primitive nature of the conditions
shocked Edward, who until now had not the slightest notion
of the poverty-stricken rural existence which enveloped those
Christians who chose not to settle in and around the capital
town of Monrovia. Men, women and children appeared to
be living alongside hog, goat and fowl as though family
members, and Edward had never before witnessed such scenes

of squalor, not even on the worst-run plantations in his native America.

Night fell quickly, the sky bereft of stars, the moon hidden behind drifting clouds. Fires were lit and the bush closed in as though a cloak were being draped around them. Madison left Edward alone with the native, and withdrew to negotiate for some shelter in which they might pass the night. An exhausted Edward slumped to the ground and removed the offending boot. Madison soon returned and informed his former master that there was only one small hut available, and they had been encouraged to share it. However, continued Madison, if his former master wished, he would happily sleep outside with the native. Edward would have none of this. Madison sat down on the dirt beside Edward and reached for a gourd of water. He drank deeply and then enquired if Edward were hungry, for the settlers would soon be roasting a goat. Pleading excessive fatigue, Edward insisted that he simply wished, if possible, to retire. Madison put the gourd to one side and, sensing the white man's discomfort, he helped him to his feet and together they crossed the strangely quiet village until they reached their lodgings. Once there, Madison deposited Edward at the mouth of the wooden hut, and then he moved off to relieve himself in the bush. Edward watched Madison's dark, glistening, sweat-filmed skin until his former slave was swallowed up whole by the blackness of the night.

When Madison returned, Edward was already undressed and basking in the glow of the lamp. Two straw cots lay next to each other, and an uneasy Madison looked around at the personal articles which littered the hut. In order that he might mask his discomfort, Madison spoke quietly as he unbuttoned his clothes. He asked Edward if there were any real purpose to their visit in a practical sense, or if this was nothing more than a tribute to Nash? Or perhaps a promise that was being kept? Edward listened intently to Madison, his eyes fixed upon his former slave. Madison removed his shirt. And then Edward shared with Madison his intention of taking the children of Nash Williams back to America and offering them the possibility of a proper Christian life amongst civilized people. Madison turned away and said nothing in reply. Outside the hut the nocturnal screeching and sawing began to build towards its terrifying nightly pitch. Edward asked the semi-clad Madison if he thought the children would return with him, and how many there were, and how many wives did Nash truly possess? Madison drank in all of these questions, and then turned back and stared directly into the face of his former master. Half of Edward's face lay shrouded in thick shadow, the other half changed hue and shape according to the nature of the dancing flame. As Madison moved to answer this volley of questions, Edward reached up his hand in a gesture of silence, and then leaned forward and took Madison's hands in his own. He spoke softly to Madison of how far he felt from home, from those like himself, and how he desired to be once more among his own people, both white and colored. Madison stared back and said nothing in reply. And then he felt the pressure increase upon his hands, and Madison took this as a signal to speak. 'No,' he said. The word echoed around the small hut, its weight and purpose obscuring the sounds of nature without. And then, after what seemed an eternity, Edward Williams gave up Madison's hands and lay back on his straw cot. covert

Shortly before noon the following day, the native helmsman leapt nimbly from the canoe and hoisted it up and on to a narrow strip of shingle. On the river bank lay scattered the rusting remains of tools and old field equipment. Edward and Madison waded ashore. They stood at the water's edge and listened to the strange creaking of the trees. Then Edward watched as his former slave found a secure footing and hoisted himself, by means of a strong vine, up and on to the summit of the muddy bank. With some aid from both the native and Madison, Edward was able to follow. There, spread before him, he could now see the litter of brown cones that

constituted the final Nash Williams settlement. Madison took
the lead and ushered Edward forward and into the unkempt
filth of the place. Everywhere he turned, Edward's eyes were
assaulted by natives who squatted idly, their bodies resting
awkwardly on their foundations, like their infantile shacks.
Edward attempted to paint his face with a thinly benevolent
smile, but realized that he was ill-equipped to disguise his
true feelings of disgust in the midst of this specter of peopled
desolation. A seemingly undisturbed Madison shepherded
Edward through the dried and drying mud, until they stood
outside of the *house* of Nash Williams. Madison pointed at the
straw grass hovel, encouraging his former master to enter, but
Edward stepped back in revulsion. What could possibly have
occurred in the Christian soul of his Nash Williams to have
encouraged him to make peace with a life that surely even these
heathens considered contemptible? Again Madison gestured to
Edward that there was nothing to block his path should he
choose to step forward and enter, but Edward recoiled. His
eyes climbed to the sun, which had now reached its highest
point in the sky, and for some moments they stood together in
silence. Then Madison pulled an over-large handkerchief from
his pocket, and dabbed at his damp brow. Edward looked
across at his former slave, and hoped that this man might
usher him towards some understanding of the disorder that
lay hereabouts. But Madison had about his person an air of
nonchalance. And then it struck Edward with a terrible force.
He was alone. He had been abandoned. Madison would not
even meet his eyes. 'Madison?' His former slave ignored him.
Recognizing the hopelessness of his predicament, Edward
opened his mouth and drew deeply of the foul air. He decided
that he would sing a hymn, in order that he might calm his
beleaguered mind. The natives stared at him, and watched as
the white man's lips formed the words, but no sound was
heard. Still, Edward continued to *sing* his hymn. The natives
looked on and wondered what evil spirits had populated this
poor man's soul and dragged him down to such a level of

abasement. Their hearts began to swell with the pity that one feels for a fellow being who has lost both his way and his sense of purpose. This strange old white man. Madison turned away.

II

West

Curling herself into a tight fist against the cold, Martha huddled in the doorway and wondered if tonight she might see snow. Beautiful. Lifting her eyes without lifting up her head, she stared at the wide black sky that would once more be her companion. White snow, come quickly. A tall man in a long overcoat, and with a freshly trimmed beard, chin tucked into his chest, looked down at her as he walked by. For a moment she worried that he might spit, but he did not. So this was Colorado Territory, a place she had crossed prairie and desert to reach. Hoping to pass through it quickly, not believing that she would fall over foolish like a lame mule. Old woman. They had set her down and continued on to California. She hacked violently. Through some atavistic mist, Martha peered back east, beyond Kansas, back beyond her motherhood, her teen years, her arrival in Virginia, to a smooth white beach where a trembling girl waited with two boys and a man. Standing off, a ship. Her journey had been a long one. But now the sun had set. Her course was run. *Father, why hast thou forsaken me?*

Lucy would be waiting for her in California, for it was she who had persuaded Martha Randolph that there were colored folks living on both sides of the mountains now. Living. According to Lucy, colored folks of all ages and backgrounds, of all classes and colors, were looking to the coast. Lucy's man had told her, and Lucy in turn had told Martha. Girl, you sure? Apparently, these days colored folks were not heading west prospecting for no gold, they were just prospecting for a new life without having to pay no heed to the white man and his

ways. Prospecting for a place where things were a little better
than bad, and where you weren't always looking over your
shoulder and wondering when somebody was going to do
you wrong. Prospecting for a place where your name wasn't
'boy' or 'aunty', and where you could be a part of this country
without feeling like you wasn't really a part. Lucy had left
behind a letter for her long-time friend, practically begging her
to come out west and join her and her man in San Francisco.
It would make the both of us happy. And although Martha
still had some trouble figuring out words and such, she could
make out the sense in Lucy's letter, and she reckoned that's
just what she was going to do. Pioneer. She was going to stop
her scrubbing and washing. Age was getting the better of her
now, and arthritis had a stern hand on all parts of her body. She
would pioneer west. Martha pulled her knees up towards her
and stretched out a hand to adjust the rags around her feet. She
blocked up the holes where the wind was whistling through.
Stop. The doorway protected her on three sides, and she felt
sure that she should be able to sleep here without disturbing
anyone. Just leave me be. But she felt strangely beyond sleep.
As though her body were sliding carelessly towards a kind of
sleep. Like when she lost Eliza Mae. Moma. Moma.

Martha unglued her eyes and stared up into the woman's
face. 'Do you have any folks?' It had started to snow now.
Early snow, huge, soft snowflakes spinning down out of the
clear, black sky. 'You must be cold.' It was dark and, the
woman aside, there was nobody else in sight. When they had
set her down here, they had told her that this was Main Street,
as though this information freed them of any responsibility.
But she did not blame them. A few saloons, a restaurant, a
blacksmith, a rooming house or two, indeed this was Main
Street. 'I have a small cabin where you can stay the night.'
Martha looked again at the woman who stood before her in a
black coat, with a thick shawl thrown idly across her shoulders
and a hat fastened tightly to her head. Perhaps this woman had
bought her daughter? Was Eliza Mae living here in Colorado

Territory? There was no reason to go clear to California if Eliza Mae were here in Colorado Territory. Eliza Mae returned to her? 'Can you get up?' The woman stretched out her gloved hand and Martha stared hard at it. Eliza Mae was gone. This hand could no more lead her back to her daughter than it could lead Martha back to her own youthful self. A small cabin. This woman was offering her some place with a roof, and maybe even a little heating. Martha closed her eyes. After countless years of journeying, the hand was both insult and salvation, but the woman was not to know this. 'Please, take my hand. I'm not here to harm you. I just want to help. Truly.' Martha uncurled her fingers and set them against the woman's hide-bound hand. The woman felt neither warm nor cold. 'Can you stand by yourself?' Inside of herself, Martha laughed. Can this woman not see that they abandoned me? At least they had shown some charity and not discarded her upon the plains. But stand by herself? Martha Randolph. Squatting like a filthy bag of bones. Watching the snow. Don't know nobody in these parts. Barely recognizing herself. No ma'am, she thought. I doubt if I'll ever be able to stand by myself again. But no matter. I done enough standing by myself to last most folks three or four lifetimes. Ain't nothing shameful in resting now. No ma'am, nothing shameful at all. She squeezed. The woman's hand squeezed back. 'Can you stand by yourself?' Martha shook her head.

I look into his eyes, but his stare is constant and frightens me. He shows no emotion. 'Lucas?' He turns from me and scrapes the wooden chair across the floor. He sits heavily upon it. He lifts his hands to his head and buries his face in his cupped and calloused palms. Eliza Mae runs to me and clutches the hem of my dress. The light in the lamp jumps and the room sways, first one way and then the next. I pull Eliza Mae towards me and hide her small body in the folds of my dress. Lucas looks up. He opens his mouth to speak. His face is tired, older than his thirty-five years. The weight of yet another day in the field sits heavily upon him. But not just this. I run my hand across Eliza Mae's matted hair. On Sunday I will pull the comb through the knots and she will scream. Outside, I can hear the crickets, their shrill voices snapping, like twigs being broken from a tree. 'Master dead.' Eliza Mae looks from me to her father, then back to me. Poor child, she does not understand. 'Lucas, we going to be sold?' Lucas lowers his eyes.

The sun is at its highest point. The overseer is looking across at me, so again I bend down and start to pick. Already I have the hands of a woman twice my age, the skin beaten, bloodied and bruised, like worn-out leather. The overseer rides his horse towards me, its legs stepping high, prancing, almost dancing. He looks down at me, the sun behind him, framing his head, forming a halo. He raises his whip and brings it down on my arm. I don't hear the words that fall from his mouth. I simply think, Master dead. What now? I bend down and again I start to pick. I can still feel his eyes upon me. And the sun. And now the horse is turning. It dances away from me.

I stand with the rest of the Virginia property. Master's nephew, a banker from Washington, is now our new master. He has no interest in plantation life. He holds a handkerchief to his face and looks on with detachment. Everything must be sold. The lawyer grabs the iron-throated bell and summons the people to attention. Then the auctioneer slaps his gavel against a block of wood. I fall to my knees and take Eliza Mae in my arms. I did not suckle this child at the breast, nor did I cradle her in my arms and shower her with what love I have, to see her taken away from me. As the auctioneer begins to bellow, I look into Eliza Mae's face. He is calling out the date, the place, the time. Master would never have sold any of us. I tell this to my terrified child. Slaves. Farm animals. Household furniture. Farm tools. We are to be sold in this order. I watch as Lucas soaks a cloth in cold water. He comforts me and places it first on my forehead, and then on that of his child. Last night he came to me, his eyes grown red with drink. He confessed that death would be easier. This way we are always going to be wondering. Always worrying. His voice broke and he choked back the remaining words. Then he took me in the circle of his arms and laid me down. Until the old horn blew to mark the start of a new day.

Farmers have come from all over the county. A fun-seeking crowd, ready for haggling, but amongst them I see the lean-faced men. The traders, with their trigger-happy minds, their mouths tight and bitter. I try not to look into anybody's eyes. The auctioneer is dressed formally. Dark vest, colorful cutaway coat. He continues to yell. Now, as he does so, he motions towards us with his gavel. Then he slaps this instrument against the wooden block with a thud. Now again he gestures towards us. My throat is dry. Eliza Mae moves restlessly, so I take her hand. She cries. I pinch her to quiet her. I am sorry, but it is for her own good. The auctioneer beckons forward the traders. They look firstly at the men. A trader prods Lucas's biceps with a stick. If a trader buys a man, it is down the river. To die. That much we all know. The families in need of domestics, or the farmers in need of breeding wenches, they look across at us and wait their turn. I am too old for breeding. They do not know that I would also disappoint. My Eliza Mae holds on to me, but it will be to no avail. She will be a prime purchase. And on her own she stands a better chance of a fine family. I want to tell her this, to encourage her to let go, but I have not the heart. I look on. The auctioneer cries to the heavens. A band strikes up. A troupe of minstrels begins to dance. Soon the bidding will begin. 'Moma.' Eliza Mae whispers the word over and over again, as though this were the only word she possessed. This one word. This word only.

Martha leaned against the woman and peered into the small, dark room. Still cold. Through the half-light, she saw the single bed, the mattress rolled back and revealing an ugly grid of rusty wire. Then she felt the woman's gentle touch guiding her across the room and into a hard-backed wooden chair. Like a child. Martha sat and watched as the woman first lit the lamp and then quickly made up the bed, stretching a clean sheet tight like a drumskin across its length and breadth. Having done so, she helped Martha the two paces across the room and set her down to rest upon the corner of the bed. Martha's right eye was clouding over, but she could make out the woman's motions as she now attempted to fire some life into the pot-bellied stove. She failed, and bestowed a sad smile upon Martha. Girl, don't worry. Don't worry yourself. The woman reached for the pitcher and poured a glass of water. 'Here, take it and drink. Are you cold?' Martha dragged her tongue around her swollen lips. Then she took the water and held the glass between both hands. She swallowed deeply, and as she did so the woman knelt and began to remove the wet rags that swaddled Martha's feet. No. Please. Martha closed her eyes.

She could only once remember being this cold. That was on that miserable December day that she had crossed the Missouri, riding in the back of the Hoffmans' open wagon. When they arrived on the western shore, Martha, by now gaunt and tired, having travelled clear from Virginia with only the briefest of stops, stepped down into the iciness that was a Kansas winter. Did they buy me to kill me? All her belongings dangled in a bundle that she held in one hand. She no longer possessed either a husband or a daughter, but her memory of their loss was clear. She remembered the disdainful posture of Master's nephew, and the booming voice of the auctioneer. She remembered the southern ladies in their white cotton sun bonnets and long-sleeved dresses, and the poorer farmers who hoped to find a bargain, their bony mules hitched to lame carriages. The trader who had prodded Lucas with a stick bought him for a princely sum. But Martha held on to some hope, for Lucas was a man who never failed to make friends with dogs. He charmed them with his dark, gentle voice. Lucas was not a man to let his body fetch up in flinty, lonely ground. Eliza Mae was sold after Martha. The

Hoffmans could no doubt detect in their purchase a powerful feeling towards this girl, so they had bundled Martha into their wagon and left quickly. They had made their transaction, and the festivities would run their natural course without them. Goodbye, everybody. Once they had passed out of sight, the woman offered Martha a lace handkerchief, which Martha ignored.

Within the year, the Hoffmans had decided to sell up and leave Virginia. They had decided to settle outside of the city of Kansas, in a part of the country which was young and promising for pioneers. Good roads provided easy access to the back country, and new arrivants were permitted to purchase land from the United States government at a cost of two dollars an acre. Mr Eugene Hoffman intended to do a little farming on his five-acre homestead, and he had ambitions of building up a herd of forty cattle and a dozen or so hogs. Cleo Hoffman, her training having prepared her for a life of teaching music, mainly the piano, was equally optimistic. Deeply religious people, they were sadly without children. In this Kansas, Martha sometimes heard voices. Perhaps there was a God. Perhaps not. She found herself assaulted by loneliness, and drifting into middle age without a family. Voices from the past. Some she recognized. Some she did not. But, nevertheless, she listened. Recognizing her despair, Mr and Mrs Hoffman took Martha with them to a four-day revival by the river, where a dedicated young circuit rider named Wilson attempted to cast light in on Martha's dark soul. Satan be gone. The young evangelist preached with all his might, but Martha could find no solace in religion, and was unable to sympathize with the sufferings of the son of God when set against her own private misery. She stared at the Kansas sky. The shield of the moon shone brightly. Still she heard voices. Never again would the Hoffmans mention their God to Martha.

And then one morning, Mr Hoffman called the graying Martha to him. She knew this would eventually happen, for the crops were not selling, and once again the cattle had come back from market. A merciful market where nothing would sell. Martha had overheard them arguing with each other at the dinner table. Mr Hoffman looked at Martha, and then down at his hands which were folded in front of him. 'We have to go west, Martha. To where there is work for us. Kansas is still too young.' He paused. 'We are going to California, but we shall have to sell you back across the river in order that we can make this journey.' Martha's heart fell like a stone. No. 'We shall do all that we can to ensure that you are rewarded with good Christian owners.' No. He continued to speak, but Martha did not hear a word he uttered. Across the river to Hell. Eventually she asked, 'When?' She was unable to tell whether she had cut him off by speaking. Mr Hoffman cleared his throat. 'Next week, Martha.' He paused and looked up at her. 'I'm sorry.' This appeared to be his way of apologizing and dismissing her at the same time. It was possible that he was sorry. For himself. Martha was not sure if she should or could leave. Then Mr Hoffman climbed to his feet. 'You can leave, Martha.'

That night, Martha packed her bundle and left the house. For where, she was not sure (don't care where), being concerned only with heading west (going west), away from the big river (away from Hell), and avoiding nigger traders who would gladly sell her back over the border and into Missouri. The dark night spread before her, but behind the drifting clouds she knew the sky was heavy with stars. (Feeling good.) And then Martha heard the barking of dogs, and she tumbled into a ditch. (Lord, give me Lucas's voice.) She waited but heard nothing, only silence. (Thank you.) Eventually, Martha climbed to her feet and began to run. (Like the wind, girl.) Never again would she stand on an auction block. (Never.) Never again would she be renamed. (Never.) Never again would she belong to anybody. (No sir, never.) Martha looked over her shoulders as she ran. (Like the wind, girl.) And then, later, she saw dawn announcing its bold self, and a breathless Martha stopped to rest beneath a huge willow tree. (Don't nobody own me now.) She looked up, and through the thicket of branches she saw the morning star throbbing in the sky. As though recklessly attempting to preserve its life into the heart of a new day.

The woman poured Martha another glass of water, which Martha held tightly, as though trying to pull some heat from the wet glass. Still cold. She stared at Martha, who noticed now that this woman had the defensive, watchful eyes of a person who had never lost control of herself. The woman loosened her shawl, revealing a gold necklace at her throat. Still cold. 'Should I leave you now?' Beneath the hat, Martha could detect a shock of gray hair, but she was unclear as to whether or not the woman was trying to conceal it. Then somebody moved outside, their shadow darkening the line of light at the bottom of the closed door, their weight firing the floorboards. No. Martha's breath ran backwards into her body. For a moment, she was unsure if she would ever have the power to expel it and then, against her will, she burst in a quiet sigh. Eliza Mae. Come back for her? 'Shall I leave you now?' 'No.' Martha released the word, without quite understanding why she had done so. Then, as the woman sat on the edge of the mattress, and Martha felt the bed lurch beneath her, she regretted the generosity of her invitation. The woman was making herself at home.

I put down the plates in front of these men and stand back. They do not take their eyes from me. 'Thank you, ma'am.' The one with the blue eyes speaks quietly. The other two are in his shadow. They all dress alike in fancy attire; silver spurs, buckskin pants, and hats trimmed with rattlesnake skin. These three unshaven men, who sit uncomfortably in my restaurant. My other customers have left. They have driven away my customers. The truth is, there was only one other customer. These days, I am lucky to set eyes on more than six or seven a day. Colored men don't appear to be riding the trail like they used to. Coming in here with their kidneys and lungs all ruined, spitting blood, arms and legs broken over and over. Even the toughest of them lasted only a few years, but now it looks like their day is done. 'Anything else I can get you?' They still haven't touched their food. 'When's he due back, ma'am?' I run my hands down the front of my dress. They are more worn than ever, not just from the cooking, but from the washing and cleaning. It is almost ten years now since I arrived in Dodge and set up laundering clothes, then cooking some, then doing both when Lucy agreed to come in and help me out. 'He'll be back at dusk.' My mind turns to Lucy in the back. Waiting for me. Needing my help. We have a large order of washing needs finishing up before morning. 'Dusk?' He lets the word fall gently from his lips, as though he were the first man to coin such a term. I nod.

There used to be four of them when they last came up the trail. I don't remember the fourth man, but I know that there used to be a fourth. They arrived as four, but left as three. This time they have arrived as three and will leave as three. They tried to cheat Chester while playing poker in the saloon bar, but Chester, in his gentle manner, sneaked a little piece of chewing tobacco into his mouth and pointed up their ways. According to the sheriff, the fourth man, the scoundrel amongst them, he drew the first gun. The sheriff let Chester go. Gunplay is second nature to Chester. Their food is getting cold. One man picks up his fork and chases the potatoes through the gravy and around the plate a little. I know he wants to eat. He is waiting for the signal with mounting hunger. I tell the man that I have to go out back now, but he simply stares at me with those blue eyes. I tell him that I have clothes to wash. I offer him this information almost as a gift. He looks across at his friends, who can barely restrain themselves. They want to eat. He waves a dismissive hand in my face. Then, as though it is not important, he reaches into his pocket and throws a few bills on to the table top. He tells me that they will leave when they have finished. That they will wait out front for Chester.

I lift the dripping pile of clothes out of the boiler and drop
them into the tub. I feel Lucy's eyes upon me, but I will not
turn to face her. I am hot. I wipe my brow with the sleeve of
my dress, and then again I bend over and try to squeeze more
water from the shirts. She puts her hand on my shoulder, this
woman who has been both friend and sister to me. She puts her
hand on my shoulder and presses. She says nothing, and I still
do not turn around. I continue to knead the clothes between
my tired fingers. 'Martha,' she begins. 'Martha, child.' I turn
to look at her. I drop the clothes and wrap my wet arms around
her, and she pulls me close. I begin to sob. She says, 'You must
go to Chester and warn him.' I listen to her, but we both know
that it is too late. Even as she insists that I should leave now,
she clasps me tighter.

I stand in the street. I see him in the distance, the dust
clouding slowly around him as his horse, frame bent, head
low, ambles out of the sunset and into the shadow that marks
the beginning of the street. And they see him too. All three
of them. They jump down from the rail. Lucy stands in the
open doorway and looks on. I had only been in Dodge a few
weeks when he came to me with his clothes to be laundered.
He came back every Tuesday afternoon, as regular as sunset,
but he barely spoke. Tipped his hat, always called me 'ma'am',
never asked me for no money, or no credit, or no nothing. And
then one day he told me that his name was Chester, that he was
a wrangler on a ranch just outside of Dodge, that nobody could
top off a bad horse like him, that he could smell loneliness like a
buffalo could smell water. I told him, I didn't need no help, I
just needed some companionship, that's all. He looked at me
with a broad, knowing look, a look that could charm the gold
out of a man's teeth, and asked if I wanted to move in with him
into his store. I asked him what he sold, and he told me that
he didn't sell a 'damn thing', but, there was plenty of room if
I wanted to open up a business. He said that if we were going
to prospect for happiness together, then he figured we ought
to try and make a little money too. I told Chester that I didn't

think I could make him no babies no more. He smiled and said, 'I got babies some place that I ain't been no kind of father to. Figure it's best if I don't bother with no more baby-making.' He paused. 'I guess you noticed I ain't one to dress to impress the local belles.' Then he laughed some, till the tears streamed down his sweet chocolate face. That same afternoon, I pulled off my apron, pulled on a clean, calico dress, pinned down my hair with a bandana, and moved everything to Chester's place, which turned out to be a proper store. Chester said he won it in a card game from a storekeeper who had headed south to Mexico with everything he owned in his pockets. He claimed that, to begin with, some folks didn't take to the idea of a colored owning decent property, but by and by people let him be. He sat amongst the lumber stores, merchants, watchmakers, carpenters, blacksmiths, mechanics, medical men and lawyers, trading nothing.

I soon set up in business concocting stews and soups for weary, half-starved colored men who had long since spent their trail rations. Vegetables and livestock, grown and raised in and around Dodge, appeared on the market. Beans, potatoes and onions at twenty-five cents a pound, beef at quarter the price, and large, plump turkeys at less than two dollars a piece. War came and war went and, almost unnoticed, the Union toppled. For a week or so, all lines were forgotten as Dodge toasted the victors in liquor until most folks could no longer hold a glass. I was free now, but it was difficult to tell what difference being free was making to my life. I was just doing the same things like before, only I was more contented, not on account of no emancipation proclamation, but on account of my Chester. I look down the street and see him coming yet closer, his shoulders square, his head held high. For ten long years, this man has made me happy. For ten long years, this man has made me forget – and that's a gift from above. I never thought anybody could give me so much love, even without trying, without appearing to make any effort, without raising no dust about it. Just steering and roping, and whatever manner of business he felt like seeing to in the days, watching the sunset at dusk, and a little whiskey and cards at night. Always there when I needed him. I glance at Lucy, whose face is a picture of fear. I want to tell her, 'Don't worry, Lucy.' And then the shots ring out and Chester slumps from the saddle, but his foot gets caught up in the stirrup. His horse stops and lets Chester fall respectfully to the ground. Three brave men with pistols smoking, and Lucy screaming.

Lucy brings the candle to my room and sits on a wicker chair. She has not yet stopped crying. I have not begun. 'We can go up to Leavenworth,' she says. 'I hear that the colored troops in the Fort are always looking for somebody to wash and clean for them. And plenty of colored folks still figuring to come across the Missouri and into Kansas.' I stare back at her, but say nothing. 'We can't stay here, Martha.' I know this. I know that I will never again be happy in fast-loving, high-speeding Dodge. Not without Chester. And the restaurant. 'We can take our business to Leavenworth, establish a laundry.' I nod in agreement. Then I ask her. 'Lucy,' I say, 'did I ever tell you that I had a daughter?' She looks back at me in astonishment.

Again she asked Martha if she was cold, and this time Martha could not hold back the sad confession that, despite this woman's efforts, her body remained numb. Too late. The woman smiled, then stood and stoked at the stove, but her gesture was one of idle hope. Too late. On top of the stove sat a great iron kettle which reminded Martha of the one back east, twenty-five years ago, in Virginia, which rang like a bell when you struck it. And if you put the tips of your fingers against it, you could feel the black metal still humming long after the kettle had ceased its song. Martha used to catch rainwater in it, the same rainwater with which she would wash Eliza Mae's matted hair. Keep still, girl. Such misery in one life. She looked at the palms of her hands where the darker skin had now bled into the lighter, and she wondered if freedom was more important than love, and indeed if love was at all possible without somebody taking it from her. Her tired mind swelled and surged with these difficult thoughts, until it pained her to think. The woman finally stopped her stoking. Martha could feel the tears welling up behind her eyes. 'Can I help?' No, you must go. 'Are you all right?' No. Please go. 'I'm sorry about the stove.' No. No. No. Martha stifled a sob.

It seemed another age now, although in truth it was only two months ago that Lucy, her hair in a wrap, had come to her in the small, two-roomed cabin that they shared, and broken the news of her impending marriage. It had been a dark night, the solitary light from a candle teasing the two friends with the twin possibilities of both warmth and security. Not that Lucy's news came as any surprise to Martha, for she had long been aware of her friend's feelings for the colored man from the dry goods store. Tubs and boilers no longer had a hold on Lucy's mind, and now she would be escaping them by marrying this man who had built himself a storey and a half house from the profits of selling that boom-town, sure-fire money-maker at a dollar a pound: nails. Martha took Lucy's hands in her own, and told her that she was pleased, and that Lucy must not, under any circumstances, worry over her. With this said, she encouraged Lucy to begin packing if she was going to leave, as planned, in the morning. Lucy levered herself out of her chair and began to address herself to the tasks at hand, while an ailing Martha sat basking in the glow of the candle and watched her. These days, Martha's old body was overburdened, and seldom did she pass an afternoon without a few cat-naps. By evening her feet and ankles were so swollen that she had to use both hands to pull off her shoes, and her undergarments now grew strangely tight during the days, her underskirt band often cutting into her waist. She desperately needed to rest, but she had determined that Lucy must never see the evidence of her malaise. And certainly not now. Lucy was to leave with a clear conscience, but not before Martha had herded her into the picture-making man's studio and ordered her to sit still. She watched her friend as she continued to gather up her few belongings, and Martha began to laugh quietly to herself.

A week later, the man came into the cabin outhouse, his arms burdened down with a bundle of heavy flannel shirts and coarse pants that needed laundering. Such visits were becoming less common, for either men seemed to be getting accustomed to giving their own garments the soap and water treatment, or Martha had serious competition from some place that she had not, as yet, heard about. The conversation that he struck up with Martha was a generous one, in that he desired to know if she could possibly manage this load by herself. Well, excuse me, mister. Was there anybody else in town to whom he might turn? Feigning ignorance of what he might be implying, Martha took the clothes and assured him that they would be ready for him whenever he needed them. This was just as well, he said, for he would soon be leaving for California with a group of colored pioneers. He informed her of this fact as though it were something that one ought to be proud of, and with this announcement delivered, he tipped his hat and wished her good day. After he left, Martha thought long and hard about her own prospects. The many years of her life with Lucy in this two-roomed cabin were now at an end, and although this Leavenworth had suited her, despite its numerous saloons, billiard parlors and houses of joy, Martha felt that she must leave. Not that Leavenworth was either violent or dangerous. In fact, the townsmen had established a liking for law and order, and introduced codes that were rigidly enforced by deputies and marshals, which meant that in this town the fast gun was not the law. But although Leavenworth was free of the turbulence of Dodge, and in spite of the fact that her years here had been peaceful, if somewhat lonely, Martha had a strange notion that she, too, must become a part of the colored exodus that was heading west. Lucy had left behind a letter, not so much inviting

Martha to come out and join her and her future husband in
San Francisco, but begging her to do so. Martha unfolded
the square of paper and decided to look it over one more
time. Then, when she had finished, she blew out the lamp
and sat quietly in the dark. Eliza Mae was once again back
in her mind, not that her lost child had ever truly vanished.
Perhaps her girl-child had pioneered west?

When, some days later, the man returned for his clean
and well-ironed garments, Martha eyeballed him directly
and announced that she, too, would be coming along. She
deliberately did not ask, but he, with equal deliberation, did
not respond. So once again, Martha informed him of her
decision, and only now did he put down the clothes and
begin to explain why this would not be possible. He advised
Martha that this was to be a long and difficult journey, with
at least twenty wagons, and they would have to cope with
what the Indians called 'crazy weather', both blizzards and
heat. Martha simply stared back at the man, forcing him to
continue. 'We'll be following stream beds most of the way,
but you never know.' He shrugged his shoulders. 'And we'll
likely be called upon to walk, for the wagons will use every
ounce of space for food, water, tools, and so on.' Martha
found herself borrowing courage from this conversation, the
way she had seen some men do from tequila. 'My role will
be to cook for you,' she said. 'I won't be a burden, but I don't
have no savings.' She went on, assuring him that she knew
about wild and dangerous country, and had many times seen
horses and oxen shot that had broken their legs, and watched
as the trailriders made soup out of their hides and bones.
She claimed that she had been aboard wagons that had fallen
clean apart, that she knew sagebrush and sidewinders like they
were her kin, and the shifting sands and whirling dust of the
cactus-shrouded world would suit her just dandy. 'I'm afraid
of nothing,' said Martha, 'least of all Indians or hard times.
Colored folks generally got to be obligated to white folks to
get clear to California, but you colored pioneers are offering

me a chance. You let me work my fare out and I'll cook, wash clothes, and powerfully nurse to the sick and ailing. And I ain't fussy about sleeping on no bare ground. I done it plenty of times before, had the beaten hardness of the earth for a bed and the sky for covering.' The man looked blankly at her, but Martha, anxious that she should not be fooled, pressed on and asked after him when they proposed leaving. 'The day after tomorrow,' he said, his voice low, his expression now one of confusion. 'I'll be ready,' said Martha, tearing at her apron. 'And you just tell your people that you done found a cook.' He smiled weakly, then turned and left, his arms laden with clean laundry. My daughter. The energy of youth once more stirred within her. I know I'm going to find my child in California.

But the woman who now stood above Martha, casting pitiful glances, was not her daughter. Eliza Mae? 'I'll leave you now,' she said. 'But you must expect to receive me in the morning.' You must expect to receive me? Did she mean by this to suggest that Martha had some choice over their arrangement? That she could, if she so wished, choose not to receive her in the morning? Martha watched the woman back slowly out of the cold room. Thank you. She left Martha alone. Sickness had descended upon her and she was unable to respond. Martha felt the sadness of not possessing a faith that could reassure her that, having served her apportioned span, she would now be ushered to a place of reunion. She looked through the cracked window-pane. Dawn was some hours off, back east, approaching slowly. To be reunited. The town of Denver was mantled in a deep snow, the arms of the trees sheathed in a thin frost, the same thin frost that enveloped Martha's faithless heart.

The evening sky is streaked with red and yellow. I watch as the sun prepares to go down beneath the horizon. To my left, there is panic. Voices begin to climb. A pioneer has broken an ox by driving it too hard. It has to be slaughtered, but at least there will be fresh meat. He ignores this commotion and stands before me with frustration written across his face. I know that I have slowed down their progress. It is this that he wishes to talk with me about. He rolls a cigarette, his fingers clammy and stiff, and then he gestures me to rest upon the hide-bottom chair. He is a man who speaks as much with his hands as his voice. I had noticed this when he first came in with his bundle of flannel shirts and coarse pants. 'Well?' This is his beginning. I know what will follow. I look beyond him. A storm is working its way across the land. My old ears can still hear the dull rumbling of thunder.

Six weeks ago we set out across the open prairie, dust clouds rising, the noonday sun at full strength, a party of seventy colored people walking to the side of our wagons. The wagons were drawn by six oxen trained to work in pairs, animals which have a tendency to skittishness, and as such they initially frightened me. The first and rear wagons were attended to by experienced drivers, but the rest were handled by we pioneers. The idea was that I should cook for all those without family, mainly bullwhackers, all men, and this I tried to do, rustling up bacon and salt pork and any game or beast that the men might happen to shoot along the way. I made sure each wagon had ample amounts of flour, sugar, coffee and rice, and a plentiful supply of ten-gallon water kegs. Other provisions and equipment in my charge included vinegar, soap, matches, cooking utensils and field stoves. But it was never easy. Before dawn, the freezing wind ripped through our clothing and right into the marrow. At noon, and early in the afternoon, the sun often caused us serious discomforts, made worse by the type of clothing that we wore. Heavy pants and flannel shirts for the men, and high-necked, long-sleeved, dark dresses that wouldn't show the dirt for the women. At night, we drew the wagons into a circle, and camp fires were built, meals cooked, and tales told of white expeditions where cruelties were often inflicted upon colored men and women.

The wagon train soon settled into a routine where one

difficult day seemed much like the next, and where there was no discernible change to the uniform landscape. However, I felt myself growing weaker, and I tried in vain to diguise my ailments. Some days we covered ten miles across the dry grass, some days twelve or fifteen, depending upon repairs or the weather. We saw Indians, and I felt some sympathy with them, but the Indian bands kept their distance and watched, choosing not to make anything of their encounters with the dark white men. Except on one occasion, when a column of a dozen warriors, at their head a chief, rode out towards the train. Behind them came the squaws, some with papooses slung across their backs, and all around them yapped pitiful-looking dogs who would in time become food. The chief halted, as did the wagon train, and he dismounted. By means of facial expressions and gestures, he made it known that we could pass in peace. I watched as our leader rewarded him with sugar and tobacco, and he in turn was rewarded with grunts of approval. Our only other visitors were the dark, shaggy buffalo who moved at such a slow pace that it was difficult to make out their progress. Our leader forbade the men, who were tiring of my pork, to stalk and hunt these monsters, informing them that should they be *spooked* and stampede, they would happily trample all before them. The occasional deer or game bird was the only alternative to that which we carried aboard the wagons.

Ten days ago, the river source began to dwindle to a mere trickle, and water was severely rationed. I watched the oxen pulling the enormous loads with heroism, and I witnessed the equally impressive bravery of the pioneers who, dehydrated as they were, energy flowing back and forth, still managed to pursue the torture. My own state became perilous, racked as I was with exhaustion, but still I managed to keep my misery to myself. Until yesterday. When it became clear that I was unable to prepare any more meals. I had long since been relieved of laundry duties, owing to the water rationing, and I had occasionally begged a ride on a wagon while all others walked. But then, this final humiliation. Yesterday morning, under the dazzling, intense blue of the Colorado sky, the foothills of the Rockies in the distance, this frustrated man sat before me with a stern face and shared with me his water ration. Suddenly, and without warning, his face softened and he spoke. 'Today and tomorrow you will rest, Martha. Ride in Jacob's wagon on the flour sacks. Tomorrow evening we shall speak again.' He took my hand with what I imagined to be real affection.

'Well?' This is his beginning. I know what will follow. 'You must find some shelter, for you will never survive the journey to California.' I say nothing. The sun finally disappears beneath the horizon. I look across to the large fire where they are preparing the evening meal. Six weeks ago, I was one of them. But times have changed. Still, I cherish these brave people – these colored pioneers – among whom I travel. They took upon themselves this old, colored woman and chose not to put her down like a useless load. Until now. 'Tomorrow, Martha.' I nod, unable to find the words to convince him that he must not feel guilty. None of them should. I am grateful. That is all. I am simply grateful. I smile at this man who is young enough to be my son. 'Thank you,' he says. He turns away before one of us discovers words that are best left undisturbed.

At dawn, they bear me like a slaughtered hog up and into the back of a wagon. But first they have cleared out some supplies to make room for me. Other wagons will bear the burden of carrying these provisions. He approaches and tells me that I will be taken to Denver, which lies some miles off their course. If I leave now, I may reach by sunset, which will give the wagon a chance to rejoin the group within two days. It is still cold. He offers me an extra blanket, which I take. We are to peel off from the main group, myself and two men, and strike out alone. He tells me that I have nothing to be afraid of. God willing, he hopes one day to find me in California. I thank him. All about me the pioneers stir. Sunken-eyed, still tired. I nursed and fed many of them through the first trying days, forcing food and water down their throats, and rallying them to their feet in order that they might trudge ten more miles towards their beloved California. Once there, they all dream of tasting true freedom, of learning important skills, of establishing themselves as a sober and respectable class of people. This is their dream. My weakness will delay them no longer. I hear the snap of a whip, and the driver yelling a sharp, impatient phrase to his oxen. As we move off, the tears begin to course down my old face.

We pass into a town on whose outskirts stand log cabins, some finished, some unfinished, but clearly being attended to. The town is growing. As we journey on, I see stores, rooming houses and saloons. But I see only two people. Indians. I remember the day the colored troops of Leavenworth paraded Indian scalps, fingers with rings attached, and ears that had been pulled clean off. They behaved like the men whose uniforms they wore. And now the Indians disappear from view. Up here in the Rockies, my breath is short and I gasp for air. I lie back down, but cannot rediscover my previous position. And then the wagon shudders to a halt, and one of my fellow pioneers appears before me. 'This is Main Street, Miss Martha.' I look at him as he pulls his collar tight up under his chin. Behind him the wind is rising, and the sky is beginning to darken. 'We're under instructions to set you down right here and high-tail it back to the others.'

In the pre-dawn hours of an icy February morning, Martha opened her eyes. Outside it was still dark, and the snow continued to spin. A dream began to wash through her mind. Martha dreamed that she had travelled on west to California, by herself, and clutching her bundle of clothing. Once there she was met by Eliza Mae, who was now a tall, sturdy colored woman of some social standing. Together, they tip-toed their way through the mire of the streets to Eliza Mae's residence, which stood on a fine, broad avenue. They were greeted by

Eliza Mae's schoolteacher husband and the three children, who were all dressed in their Sunday best, even though this was not Sunday. A dumbstruck Martha touched their faces. Eliza Mae insisted that her mother should stay and live with them, but Martha was reluctant. All was not right. There was still no news of Lucas, and her Eliza Mae now called herself Cleo. Martha refused to call her daughter by this name, and insisted on calling her a name that her children and husband found puzzling. Soon it was time for Martha to leave, but her daughter simply forbade her mother to return east. Martha, feeling old and tired, sat down and wept openly, and in front of her grandchildren. She would not be going any place. She would never again head east. To Kansas. To Virginia. Or to beyond. She had a westward soul which had found its natural-born home in the bosom of her daughter.

Martha Randolph won't be taking any washing today. No tubs, no ironing. No cooking, either. Martha will simply sleep through the day. The woman, her cold body wrapped in her black coat, left the Denver streets which were now clad in thick snow. She opened the door and looked in upon the small colored woman, who stared back at her with wide eyes. The unsuccessful fire in the pot-bellied stove was dead. The woman gently closed in the door. Martha won't be taking any washing today. And the woman wondered who or what this woman was. They would have to choose a name for her if she was going to receive a Christian burial.

III

Crossing the River

Journal of a voyage intended (by God's permission) in the *Duke of York*, snow, from Liverpool to the Windward Coast of Africa, etc., commenced the 24th August 1752.

Officers and Seamen belonging to the *Duke of York*.
Commenced pay 24th August 1752.

NAMES	QUALITY	
James Hamilton	Master	
John Pierce	1st Mate	Discharged 21st Dec. 1752 *Fortune*
Henry Allen	Surgeon	
Francis Foster	2nd Mate	Deceased 26th April 1753
William Smith	3rd Mate	
Joseph Griffith	Carpenter	
George Davy	Boatswain	Discharged 15th Jan. 1753
William Barber	Cooper	
Thomas Gallagher	Steward	
Jonathan Swain	Cook	Deceased 14th March 1753
Mark Brown	Gunner	
Edward White	Carpenter's Mate	Deceased 23rd April 1753
Samuel Morgan	Fore the mast	
Matthew Pitts	do.	
John Lawson	do.	
Robert Lewis	do.	
Joseph Cropper	do.	Discharged 20th Nov. 1752
Richard Forrester	do.	
Edmund Fellows	do.	
Jacob Creed	do.	Discharged 20th Nov. 1752
George Robinson	do.	

NAMES	QUALITY	
Thomas Taylor	Fiddler do.	
James Whitaker	do.	
Peter Welsh	do.	
Owen Thompson	Ship's Apprentice	
Edward Gibson	do.	
Matthew Arthur	do.	Deceased 5th March 1753
John Johnson	do.	

Monday 24th August . . . At 3 p.m. cast from the pier head at Liverpool, run against the flood. At 7 p.m. moored with the sheet anchor. A light breeze and some rain . . .

Tuesday 25th August . . . All day cloudy weather, fresh gales. Four of our people, Edmund Fellows, James Whitaker, Edward Gibson and John Johnson, fixed the longboat's sails. Carpenter mended the channel bend. John Lawson fixed stoppers for the cables. Pilot boat came on board with 3 sheep, and 2 quarters of beef . . .

*

Thursday 27th August . . . All day fair weather. A brig informed us of variable winds . . .

*

Saturday 29th August At daylight this morning unmoored. High water, fresh gales about SW. For Windward and Gold Coast . . .

*

Wednesday 9th September Thick and fresh gales. Rain in the night, strong and at times very hard. Looking very dirty to the westward. At 2 p.m. came in with the sheet anchor in 10 fathoms. Saw the land of Dublin to the NW and W. In the road, His Majesty's Ship, the *African*, 3 Dutch, and another English vessel. Continues very bad weather . . .

Thursday 10th September All night northern lights flying about the wild sky. Daylight came on thick and the gale increased about WSW and West. At noon let go the starboard anchor under foot . . .

Friday 11th September . . . Begin to be sensible of a change of climate. Hazy weather. Some small rain. Indifferent smooth water . . .

★

Saturday 19th September On this morning discovered William Barber, Cooper, guilty of broaching a cask of ale reserved for cabin use and filling it with water. Put him in irons and, the facts being fully proved, ordered 12 lashes . . .

★

Tuesday 29th September . . . At 1 p.m. the land ahead proved to be the island Grand Canaries: soon after saw the peak of Tenerife at a great distance. People at work upon the cables. Carpenter began to raise the gratings of the women's room . . .

★

Monday 5th October . . . The water once again a deep sea colour. Sounded but could get no ground with 60 fathoms of line. A great many flying fish about us. Caught a small dolphin . . .

Tuesday 6th October . . . Carpenter fitted up state room to serve as a shop on the coast. Removed most of India cloth from hold into cabin. Got ship's arms chest aft. Marked off the slaves' rooms, and Carpenter and Mate set about building the bulkheads. All hands engaged. Gunner making cartridges, etc., for the carriage and swivel guns . . .

★

Sunday 11th October . . . Very variable winds and weather.

At 9 a.m. sails set with a pretty breeze. Got soundings at about 35 fathoms, white sand and black stones. Caught a small shark. By 2 p.m. a great deal of lightning and thunder. Very strong ripplings . . .

★

Tuesday 13th October . . . Saw land, Sierra Leone eastward about 3 miles. At 3 p.m. passed 4 vessels at anchor off the bar. One, *Mary*, a snow, of Liverpool is known to me. The *Halifax* of Bristol is almost slaved. The 2 others are schooners from New England. Have 14 fathoms of water, red sand. At sunset anchored in Frenchman's Bay. Fired 7 guns. The rest of the day was passed in feasting and firing.

Wednesday 14th October Fair weather. Made a trip with the yawl for water. Visited on board with Captain Williams of the *Mary*. He informed me that the *Devon* of Bristol was recently run on shore by the slaves in an insurrection and totally lost. There was loss of 11 crew. Upon my return the ship's company, to a man, complained that in my absence the Boatswain, Mr Davy, had used them ill. I thought it proper to put him in chains lest he might occasion disturbance when we get slaves on board.

Thursday 15th October . . . Corrected the Carpenter with a dozen stripes of the cat for making a commotion while fetching wood . . .

Friday 16th October In the morning I went on board Mr Sharp's shallop to Whiteman's Bay to view some slaves. Was shown 10, but bought none. Lame, old, or blind. In the afternoon ran up with the flood to the island factory. Got there a handsome dozen, paid the goods for them, and brought them up . . .

★

Wednesday 21st October . . . Came up from the Leeward the

Virtue, Morris, sloop, of Barbados. He has some 40 slaves on board in 2 months. He gives a disturbing account of trade down below. The price of slaves has run to 125 bars and upwards. Bartered with Captain Morris for 4 hogsheads of rum at 4/- per gallon . . .

★

Thursday 29th October . . . When it lies in the desk, the thermometer at 74, but when exposed to the heat of the sun it rose, at noon, to 96. I was much surprised to detect so great a difference . . .

★

Wednesday 4th November . . . Variable weather, mostly a land breeze, and in the night thunder and lightning. Discharged the Boatswain from his confinement, upon his promise of amendment . . .

Thursday 5th November . . . Last night Captain Morris's longboat came in with 10 more slaves having been 2 days gone. He pretends that the trade hereabouts is all engaged to him, but I am not an apprentice . . .

Friday 6th November . . . Dispatched Mr Pierce in the yawl with a letter for Mr Jones at Whiteman's Bay. I wish to know whether he can give me any encouragement to stay longer hereabouts. This evening he returned with a half-dozen fine man-boys, but the bars were excessive dear. According to Mr Pierce's testimony, gleaned from Mr Jones, the resident white men are all exhausted. This parcel of a half-dozen being the last of the present crop . . .

Saturday 7th November Fair weather, faint sea breeze. In the morning had a visit from some Portuguese of Pirates Bay. They brought a woman slave, whom I refused being long-breasted. I shall proceed down the coast once the longboat is repaired . . .

★

Thursday 12th November This morning set the punt on shore with Jacob Creed and George Robinson. Instead of returning on board they visited a French schooner and got drunk. Afterwards they returned to shore to fight, which when they were sufficiently tired of, attempted to come off, but the ebb being strong, and they by now too tired to pull well, they came upon the rocks. I sent Mr Foster to them, and he was obliged to slip the rope. I gave both of these *gentlemen* a good caning, and would carry them both confined in chains to the Americas but for the consideration of our being a slaving ship . . .

*

Saturday 14th November At daylight unmoored. At 10 a.m. came in the *Wanderer*, a French-built cutter in 7 weeks from London. At noon, being high water, weighed and worked down against the sea breeze . . .

*

Monday 16th November . . . Put a fresh cargo into the yawl. Left the ship before noon and rowed into shore. Was shown 11 slaves, of whom I picked 5, viz., 4 men, 1 woman. Paid what goods I had in the boat were suitable and I am to send the rest . . .

Tuesday 17th November . . . Went on shore directly to look at 4 slaves but they were all old. Rowed up the river and at dusk reached the town. No trade here at present, but they promised to immediately send word of my arrival to Mr Lewis . . .

Wednesday 18th November . . . Mr Lewis has promised me 2 dozen of the finest slaves if I will tarry a few more days. To this I agree. I return to discover the Boatswain, Mr Davy, once more very abusive and being blind drunk. I secure him in irons and am determined to deliver him up to the first man-of-war . . .

★

Friday 20th November Between 2 a.m. and 3 a.m., the watch upon deck being either asleep or consenting, 2 of the people, viz. Joseph Cropper and Jacob Creed, ran away with the yawl, though chained. At daylight she was perceived lying on shore, and I dispatched Mr Smith to bring her off before the blacks knew she was in their power, otherwise she would have cost me, I suppose, near to 100 bars. My people I do not expect to again encounter . . .

Saturday 21st November This morning had excessive rain for 2 hours with violent thunder and lightning, but, thank God, no damage ensued. By 3 p.m. Mr Lewis came aboard with the promised slaves, most being remarkably fine and sturdy. I purchased 17, viz., 12 men, 5 women. In future the day must begin with arms and sentinels, there now being above 50 slaves on board . . .

★

Tuesday 8th December . . . Sent Mr Foster in the yawl with goods for 5 slaves, that is to say close to 500 bars which in earlier times might have purchased 20. He returned at sunset in triumph, though it will not do to continue giving nearly what the slaves will fetch in the Americas, exclusive of freight and commissions, and besides the tediousness of trade and the great risk of mortality . . .

★

Thursday 10th December This morning fired 3 guns for trade, but it would appear that everybody is engaged, and the country hereabouts now full of goods. At 4 p.m. the *Fortune*, Jackson, snow, of Liverpool anchored nearby. At 7 p.m. I went aboard and dined with the frail veteran of the coast, Captain Jackson. We agreed to go downwards and take our share of trade, and assist and protect each other, for there is much villainy to the south, and it is judged precarious for a single ship in these times. Captain Jackson confesses that he has recently been obliged to part with 130 bars for a prime slave, one of his people having walked 2 days in the woods to look at him and bid. I am resolved to stop short of such extravagance . . .

★

Sunday 20th December An excessive dismal night, populated by a tornado which proved the most violent I have ever suffered. At the height of the squall the yawl broke the best chain on board, but by some miraculous gesture the two remaining ropes managed to hold her secure. We peered on, the night being so close there was no seeing unless in the glare of the lightning, and at regular intervals sought confirmation that our smaller party was still with us . . .

Monday 21st December . . . The storm having subsided, we anchored at noon in 13 fathoms of clear water and fired 3 guns. Soon after we saw the *Fortune*. As she drew nearer she began to fire minute guns, and we perceived her colours at half-mast, which we understood to be a melancholy signal of Captain Jackson's death. She anchored nearby, and the First Mate came aboard and informed me that in the midst of last night's terrible flurry the Captain had passed away most peacefully. I went on board with Mr Pierce and tendered him the command. He seemed greatly honoured by the charge. Soon after I returned to the *Duke of York* and at sunset fired 6 minute guns.

★

Wednesday 23rd December This morning Mr Pierce came on board and conveyed to me his desire to complete the loading of his cargo on some other part of the coast, his ship's crew reasoning that this part of Africa had brought them only ill-luck. To this I readily agreed. If the weather remained fair, the *Fortune* would, he announced, weigh anchor with the tide . . .

*

Friday 15th January At 8 a.m. set out in the punt to deliver
Mr Davy to HMS *Humber*, man-of-war, at Sierra Leone.
Hard rain and a great sea, that I was several times afraid that
we might be filled. Got safe round the rock by 3 p.m. and
aboard the *Humber* by 5 p.m. I discharged my Boatswain.
On my return I discovered that the Carpenter had finished
strengthening the *barricado*. 1 small girl had been added to
the cargo in my absence. Mr Allen, Surgeon, assured me I
would regard her a bargain. On a cursory glance I was able
to confirm for myself the strength of his judgement. The first
part of this night has blown fresh with a short, ugly sea . . .

[At Sea, 10th January.

My Dearest,

  I have, these past few days, been discouraged from writing
by the mighty apparatus of the seas. But being unable to hold
off and tolerate further delay, I now try my eyes by candlelight
and attempt to form characters that, I trust, will not try your
own. At present, I cannot imagine writing with pleasure to
any on land or sea but your own dear self, my head being full
of the petty concerns of this valuable vessel, and the lives of the
people who dwell hereabouts, whose fortunes are entrusted to
my care. These are, indeed, petty concerns when set against
my love for you, for I can declare, with honour, that barely
an hour of my past life comes to mind with any pleasure,
excepting valuable and precious time I have passed in your
company, and for that I think the innumerable miseries and
pains of my previous unhappy life, not a dear purchase. My
affection for you goes beyond any words I can find or use, and
I simply wish that it were possible for you to travel with me,
and strengthen my purpose in fatigue and difficulty, without
actually suffering them. How trifling they would seem to me!

But, I submit, I travel abroad in the comfortable knowledge that my better, precious part is safely at home, and though she understands absence to be painful, she knows it is so for her sake. I am engaged in active business, and have some new scene every day to relieve my mind; besides I have long been used to suffering. On the contrary, you, by marriage to one such as I, have exposed yourself to anxieties to which you were a stranger. I know you have done this willingly, and I love you all the greater for this sacrifice.

My last letter concluded abruptly, for I was ill and disconcerted by an incident in business. I feared it might give rise to bad consequences, and sadly this came to pass. I take a good deal of raillery among the sea-captains, for they *know* I have not a secure knowledge of life, and I *know* they have not. They claim I am melancholy; I tell them they have lost their wits. They say I am a slave to a single woman; I claim they are a slave to hundreds, of all qualities. They wonder at my *lack* of humour, I pity theirs. They declare they can form no idea of my happiness, I counter with knowledge that being pleased with a drunken debauch, or the smile of a prostitute, can never give one such as I pleasure. They pretend, all the while, to appeal to experience against me, but I stand firm. On my own ship such discord recently swelled into near-mutiny, for there is among my officers one in particular who sees me as little more than a *gentleman-passenger*. I had been warned, prior to our departure, that I might expect trouble in abundance from Mr Davy, the Boatswain, and he recently unleased his drunken invective on myself and others of our company, and then in a flight of madness attempted to seize the ship. But no more of this business, except to say that, indeed, all was very nearly lost, but now we are found. It seems that the disparity between my dear late father's great reputation, and my own youthful 26 years, fired some hereabouts, under the skilful guidance of Mr Davy, into a frenzy of hostility, the assumption being that I owed everything to my connections, and nothing to my own experience or abilities. But again, I say, no more of this business.

I confess that, when alone, the recollection of my past with you overpowers me with a tender concern, and such thoughts give me a pleasure, second only to that of being actually with you. I have written myself into tears, yet I feel a serenity I never imagined till I was able to call you mine. To win your love was my principal desire, and without it, all that you possessed, and might have bestowed upon me, would have seemed dull by comparison. I have the confidence that you love me, a confidence which renders me superior to all the little entertainments that might allure me, and all the difficulties which are daily thrown in my way. Whatever dangers and hardships I meet, I declare that no one has heard me complain. Those of my company who pity me because I appear not to be fond of what *they* call pleasure, know not what renders me superior to it. I was once, in earlier times, as eager as they after pleasure, but you have thoroughly refined my state, so that my sole pleasure is to dream of our future children, and our family life together. What I have in view at the end of this voyage, is so fixed in my thoughts, that to be acknowledged and rewarded by you, outweighs any hardship that I might possibly suffer.

I am, etc.
Inviolably yours.
James Hamilton.]

★

Wednesday 20th January . . . Fair weather, the thermometer reading 79 degrees. In the afternoon took the yawl in to see if any trade has come down as yet . . .

★

Friday 22nd January . . . Fresh gales of wind from the N to the NE with some rain. Bought a pair of man-boys from an African *prince*, as they are styled. Dispatched the yawl to the shore with instructions to fill a load of water . . .

★

Thursday 4th February This morning at daybreak I was saluted by the agreeable vision of my longboat, and soon after she came on board with crew well and a dozen slaves, viz., 4 men, 2 women, 1 man-boy, 1 boy (4 feet) and 4 girls (under-size). Mr Smith brought news that in the coming weeks there is likely to be an extraordinary run of trade and no competitors. Prices may fall below 100 bars in these conditions. In the evening I ordered the fiddler to play and strong liquors to be drunk. Hectic days lie ahead . . .

Friday 5th February . . . Put another cargo in the longboat and sent her and the yawl to Mr Johnson's with a charge to trade vigorously. The Carpenter seems to have rid himself of the drinking habit, and is busily extending the bulkhead of the men's room. This afternoon, bartered with a Frenchman for 2 anchors of brandy, 20 cwt of rice, and a man slave of quite unnatural proportions. Hot hazy weather.

Saturday 6th February This morning the yawl returned upon the flood tide with information that the *Robert*, a New England sloop, is down the coast with near 200 slaves on board, and that there has been an insurrection in her, in which the Chief Mate, 2 ordinary seamen, and 27 slaves were killed. The good news is that this portion of shoreline has proved fertile ground, and we can presently expect a brimming longboat. At 4 p.m. I dispatched the yawl laden with more goods . . .

★

Wednesday 17th February . . . An unwholesome land wind. Have the Surgeon and 4 more people ill of a fever. Carpenter purposefully employed in building the bulkheads in the women's room, Gunner cleaning the arms . . .

★

Saturday 27th February . . . A continual calm. At 3 p.m. weighed with the flood tide to drive downwards, but at sunset can hardly perceive we have made any advance. The Carpenter's work is complete, having constructed yet another platform in the men's room. The ship is clear enough to take the remainder of our slaves without inconvenience. This day fixed 6 swivel blunderbusses in the *barricado* which will, I hope, be sufficient to intimidate the slaves from any thoughts of an insurrection . . .

Sunday 28th February Anchored this morning in 15 fathoms. An excessive high surf upon the shore, which prevents the canoes from coming off. I left the ship in the punt and got over the bar, but not without some danger, the sea running high for so small a boat. Reached safely to the town by sunset. My great desire is to complete 50 slaves before I go downwards, and I have great reason to expect to do it here in a matter of days . . .

★

Saturday 6th March A hazy morning with both sea and land breeze. The fever has again taken hold among the crew and sadly dispatched one Matthew Arthur. Was obliged to bury him immediately, being extremely offensive. I sent the punt on shore with 6 casks to be filled with water. In the evening she returned with the water, and brought me a goat as a present from the King. We saluted him with 5 guns. It appears he is eager to go and look for trade for me . . .

Sunday 7th March Began this day with much activity. Cleared the women's room and scraped it. Watched the punt struggle over the bar as she returned for yet more provisions. Begin to be tired of waiting here, yet by all accounts this is the only place I can expect to lie without competition upon the whole coast. This evening the wind rose, and the current being very irregular the ship turns round like a top.

*

Friday 12th March At 3 a.m. unmoored, and at 9 a.m. weighed. Sailed downwards and anchored in 12 fathoms at sunset. Calm sea breeze. Perceived the canoes endeavouring to come off to us, and the blacks making a great fire upon the beach. Fired a carriage gun, and hoisted a light . . .

Saturday 13th March . . . At noon the canoes once again on board, brought 8 slaves, viz., 2 men, 1 woman, 2 boys, 3 girls. All small, the girl slaves all below 4 feet. Mr Wilson informed me that he had met with Mr Pierce's *Fortune*, and that the ship had well in excess of 300 slaves, and had not purchased above 3 in these parts, being concerned with quality. Sadly his yawl was lost here . . .

Sunday 14th March . . . At 1 p.m. the sea breeze came in and had a fine gale. Steered SE along the shore and anchored at 8 p.m. abreast the town in 13 fathoms, the natives making a great smoke upon the beach. In the road the *Charity*, Donald, a New England rum sloop, almost fully slaved. Received intelligence from Mr Donald that prices in these parts are more extravagant than ever, but I fancy he seeks to deceive me. Just before midnight departed this life the Cook, Jonathan Swain, after a week's illness. He was in a continual delirium.

Monday 15th March . . . Lay until noon in expectation of a canoe, but nobody stirred. Weighed with the evening tide . . .

*

Thursday 25th March At daylight saw a longboat on shore. She came aboard at 9 a.m., brought with her 5 slaves, 2 fine boys, and 3 old women whom I instructed them to dispose of. Had a very discouraging account of the state of affairs to Leeward, all about the river being full of an epidemical sickness that is ravaging amongst the slaves. The *Britannia*, Parsons, of London, was obliged to off before he had finished, having buried 25 on the coast. Discharged, cleaned and reloaded the small arms. At sunset saw a sloop rigged boat, standing up the coast . . .

★

Friday 2nd April . . . By the favour of Divine Providence made a timely discovery today that the slaves were forming a plot for an insurrection. Surprised 4 attempting to get off their irons, and upon further search in their rooms found some knives, stones, shot, etc. Put 2 in irons and delicately in the thumbscrews to encourage them to a full confession of those principally concerned. In the evening put 5 more in neck yokes.

★

Wednesday 7th April Weighed at daylight. Soon after saw a ship to windward come fast up with us. At noon I went on board, proved the *Highlander*, Daniel Wilkes, of London, with materials for a new fort on the Gold Coast. Informed him that I propose to take few more slaves for we are weak-handed through disease. I have in mind to engage no slaves under 4 feet. Returned in a leaking yawl . . .

Thursday 8th April . . . Hoisted the yawl upon the deck for she could hardly keep swimming alongside. Carpenter at work. He informs me he shall be obliged to remove every foot of plank in her bottom, being quite destroyed by the worms. The Surgeon informs me that 5 of our white people and some 11 slaves with the flux, but none without a prospect of recovery . . .

Friday 9th April Fair weather. Sea breeze. At 9 a.m. went on shore, but Mr Ellis not being upon the beach, I determined to follow him to his town. Bought a man from a stranger and sent him aboard. Then set out. Reached Mr Ellis just before dark. He promises if I will stay 21 days he will sell me as many more slaves as I can purchase, with good assortment, after which time I will be fully slaved.

Saturday 10th April Set out from Mr Ellis at sunrise, and got safe on board by 3 p.m. Saw 3 other vessels passing down, and feared that they might hurt my trade. Mercifully, none anchored by us. At 6 p.m. George Robinson seduced a woman slave big with child, and lay with her in view of the whole quarter deck. I put him in irons. I suspect this has not been the first affair of the kind on board. Her number is 72 . . .

★

Thursday 15th April Went on shore, met Mr Ellis, got only 7 men slaves from him. He says I must wait, for he has been as much disappointed as myself . . .

★

Saturday 17th April . . . When we were putting the slaves down this evening, one that was fevered jumped overboard (No. 97). Got him in again but he died immediately between his weakness and the salt water he had swallowed. To remain much longer on the coast may affect my interest and diminish my expected profits. I am yet unable to judge when I shall probably weigh for the Americas.

Sunday 18th April This morning perceived an English snow at anchor, run in and went on board her; the *Dolphin*, Freeman, 10 weeks from Liverpool, has been 6 days on the coast, brought me a letter from the owners which was well-received . . .

Monday 19th April Close weather with much thunder, lightning, and variable winds. At daylight had a canoe on board, with two young traders to offer their services. Matthew Coburn and Peter Ross of the river hereabouts, and I sent them back on shore with goods for rice, etc., and to look out for slaves. I grow impatient with Mr Ellis and am now determined to trade goods with any who can deliver up slaves. This afternoon the weather grew more agreeable. Loosed and aired the sails, discharged and reloaded the small arms . . .

Tuesday 20th April . . . This day buried 2 fine men slaves, Nos 27 and 43, having been ailing for some time, but not thought in danger. Taken suddenly with a lethargic disorder from which they generally recover. Scraped the men's rooms, then smoked the ship thoroughly with tar and tobacco for 3 hours, afterwards washed clean with vinegar . . .

Wednesday 21st April . . . Coburn and Ross came on board. Brought a large canoe-load of wood, but no slaves. I sent back 12 casks for water, and informed them of my desire to be supplied with more rice, and some fowls, etc. Buried a man slave (No. 8) having been about 10 days ill of an obstinate flux. This evening Mr Ellis's shallop crossed the bar and requested that I put goods in her to the amount of 1000 bars. At 1 a.m. observed John Johnson illegally entering into the state-room scuttle and stealing brandy. Clapped him in irons.

Thursday 22nd April . . . Turned Mr Johnson out of irons and gave him a smart dozen. From sunset till midnight very coarse weather, hard rain, strong gusts of wind and a very high swell. In this commotion 2 girl slaves, who have long been ill of a flux, died. Nos 117 and 127.

Friday 23rd April At sunrise, a snow and a sloop, both French, anchored at Leeward. Close dirty weather, and a great sea tumbling in. At 7 p.m. departed this life Edward White, Carpenter's Mate, 7 days ill of a nervous fever. Buried him at once. Put overboard a boy, No. 29, being very bad with a violent body flux. Have now 3 whites not able to help themselves . . .

Saturday 24th April At 8 a.m. calmed. Attended to the spare sails, discovered the rats to have done a great deal of damage. We are over-run with them, those cats we brought from

England having long since departed. Towards noon saw Mr Ellis's shallop with as much surprise as pleasure, for I had quite given her up. At 3 p.m. she came on board, brought 10 slaves, viz., 3 men, 3 women, 1 boy, 2 girls, 1 small boy. Mr Ellis excused his long stay on account of a general sickness which had seized them in the River, but he seems pretty well recovered. It appears his two partners linger at the point of death. Mr Ellis claimed to be in possession of 30 slaves, of superior quality, and he pledged them to me. He demanded 75 bars, which in these times would appear to be a good price. Trusted him with goods to induce him to return with slaves. Sent the punt in with water casks and instructions to come off with rice, yams, palm oil, etc.

Sunday 25th April . . . Mr Coburn and Mr Ross brought two small boys, under 3 feet 10 inches. Sent them in again with positive orders that we have little ones enough, at the price they now bear. Received from them twenty gallons of palm oil, 8 cwt of rice, besides yams and plantains. This afternoon, sent a grapnel to the yawl, gave her a heel each way and scrubbed her bottom. Likewise hoisted the punt in and cleaned her . .

Monday 26th April At sunrise a stern sea breeze. Instructed the Carpenter to make a new rudder to the longboat. At 8 a.m. a large ship anchored here within us. The *Mermaid*, sloop, of New York. Then came up from to Leeward, His Majesty's Ship, the *Prince Edward*, Captain Henry. Saluted him with 5 guns. This afternoon departed this life my Second Mate, Francis Foster, after sustaining the most violent fever. I am afraid his death will retard our trade, for he is very diligent, and always gained a great influence upon the natives. It stands fortunate that our ship is almost slaved. At sunset buried Mr Foster. Hoisted the colours to half-mast, fired a dozen minute guns. Will send the punt to the *Prince Edward* on the morning tide.

[West Africa, 25th April.

My Dearest,

These last few days have been amongst the most fatiguing I can ever recall. I, therefore, write to you in the hope of making some amends for this misfortune. Those, myself aside, who have experienced pleasant and agreeable evenings in your company, could never imagine the contrast between such sweet times, and the present miserable situation. I am continually assaulted by the combined noises of slaves and traders; suffocated by heat; and subjected to perpetual talking, the greater part of it to no serious purpose. Last night I managed some two hours of sleep, and I dreamed of you. I *saw* us walking together, and discoursing on the many things which have occurred since our parting. We took our repose beneath a heavily branched tree, and rehearsed that most happy of scenes, when you first gave to me your hand. I sat stupid for some time, and embarrassed you by my awkwardness. But my heart was so full, its beat heavy and irregular, that I knew not how to utter a word out. Your kindness and patience soon restored to me the use of my tongue, and we both concurred that the greater intimacies that have followed are the source of our supreme happiness. But then my dream was invaded by daylight, and the noise of people above my head broke the pleasing illusion. I submitted, most unwillingly, to a very different scene.

The principal cause of my sleeplessness, indeed, my distress, has been the unfeeling intransigence displayed by a certain Mr Ellis. At every opportunity, I ask after my dear late father, but he parries my enquiries. I have constantly demanded of him that he transport me to the very place where my late father, only two years past, lost his life, but he refuses to aid me. He can see plainly enough that I need to vent my grief, but he responds to my entreaties with the curious suggestion that my father traded not wisely, and with too much vigour. He goes on, and hints that Father cultivated a passionate hatred, instead of a commercial detachment, towards the poor creatures in his care, and he urges me to not err in this direction. But more than this he will not say, no matter how fervently I plead my case. I intimated that it was his Christian duty to let me set my eyes upon my father's resting place, but Mr Ellis scorned the idea of any of my name claiming kinship with the Christian faith. I confess that I was unable to respond to this charge, for indeed my father held dear to the belief that the teachings of the Lord were incompatible with his chosen occupation, and that it was folly to try and yoke together these opposites in one breast. Yet Father made no mention to me of this *hatred* that Mr Ellis claims sealed his fate. My dear, I too must confess to deep feelings of revulsion, but hatred is a word altogether too fierce to describe my natural passions, for in the same manner that a continued indulgence in this trade and a keen faith cannot reside in one breast, one heart can surely not contain the warring passions of both love and hatred. This being true, then my father's heart must surely have hardened on his final fateful voyage, either this or it was broken clean in half. It would appear that Mr Ellis seems determined to keep from me the more intimate details of this mystery, and it distresses me that his replies are so framed as to imply that my lack of years are the sole impediment to a fuller confession.

I believe my poor Second Mate, Mr Foster, will soon be gone to the sea. Besides my personal regard, I shall miss him on your account, for I have often aired my mind by talking to him about you. I judged him alone to be worthy of the subject, but beyond this person there is none with whom I would degrade your name. I will, henceforth, be forced to keep my pleasures and pains to myself, and am now likely to perform what remains of the journey alone. But I shall want no company, being contented to recall how happy I have been in yours. I went, only this morning, on deck, where the weather was perfectly still, the moon bright, and passed an hour thinking deeply of you. I indulged the hope that you were in a pleasant slumber, and free

119

from the calamitous thoughts which plague your loved one upon the seas. As long as you are favoured with health, and a moderate share of the good things of life, then I will bear all the changes of this world. You cautioned me to be watchful of my own life, for your sake, which is a most engaging argument. I know not which of us must depart first, but it is probable that one must survive the knowledge of the other's death. If it should be my lot, I cannot tell how I might bear it, for being too young to fully grieve for my dear mother, the departure of my father was the first blow, and a mighty severe one. That I loved him, is beyond doubt, although he remained strange to me in many ways, as often befits a great man. But my love for you is of an altogether different amplitude, and I fear that should you depart first, I would soon join. In the meantime, I do not expect to glide through life without meeting rubs, but I have a confidence that you love me, which I would not exchange for any consideration the world could offer. I will try Mr Ellis again, but I expect to be rebuffed, and to leave this coast with the compensatory knowledge that, despite Mr Ellis's suggestion, the reputation of my late father is secure and growing, although that of his son – the youthful *gentleman passenger* – continues to be mocked by the *salty dogs* who, I fear, will always believe my position due only to preferment. No matter. Let it suffice that I eat, drink, and sometimes sleep. I am in health, and some spirits, and shall do everything necessary to procure a future happy reconciliation, for beyond this trading community lies family life. My dear, I long to dwell safely in your arms, and revel in the imagined joys that our projected children will bless us with.

Yours, etc.
James Hamilton.]

Tuesday 27th April . . . Employed most of the day in fitting out the longboat, put goods in her for 10 slaves, and dispatched her to shore. In the afternoon loosed and aired the sails, smoked the ship with tobacco and brimstone. Sent the punt in shore to induce a large canoe to fetch more of our water casks.

Wednesday 28th April This morning buried a fine woman-girl (No. 123) of a fever which destroyed her in a single day, with much vomiting and clamour. The doctor, who is now himself recovered, grows anxious. A high swell makes the vessel labour very much. We wait upon Mr Ellis. At work mending the sails, but the rats out-do us. They forcefully bite the people if they catch them asleep. This evening, found 3 knives and similar tools in the men's room.

Thursday 29th April At 8 a.m. a stiff sea breeze. This morning put more goods and provisions in the shallop and sent her away for the river. Soon after buried a man slave (No. 39), his severe flux having baffled all our medicines. At 2 p.m. sent the yawl in over the bar. Instructions to clean and fill more water-casks, and to bring off Mr Ellis if he could be located. This evening the yawl returned with information that Mr Ellis will be here soon. Mr Coburn and Mr Ross appear to be making trade with a French sloop that stands downwards.

Friday 30th April At dawn the brig *Wanderer*, Jones, of Rhode Island, anchored within us. At 10 a.m. he came on board and informed me that downwards there were several ships and no slaves. Bought a hogshead of rum of Captain Jones. This evening a ship passed us steering downwards, showed no colours. Cleaned and reloaded the small arms. Towards midnight a great deal of lightning, and threatening clouds all around.

Saturday 1st May . . . The canoes made a single trip with water, saved a butt and a half. The frequent showers of rain deter them from making more than one trip. Cannot send

121

the yawl on account of the current which runs stronger than she can row ahead. The Cooper has finished all the casks, we simply wait. Buried a girl slave (No. 20), ill of the flux. Should I not get my capacity of slaves before the next slant of wind and current offers to go up, believe it will be best to suffer the loss, and Mr Ellis's gain, rather than spend more time to no purpose.

Sunday 2nd May . . . The season advancing fast and, I am afraid, sickness too. Almost every day one or two more taken with the flux, of which a man-boy (No. 59) died tonight. I imputed it to the English provisions, and have begun to feed them rice. Brought off 24 casks of water and 3 loads of wood, no word from Mr Ellis. A William Givens brought about 290 lbs of rice and 2 women slaves. I gave him goods, and encouraged him to procure me others if he does so in haste.

Monday 3rd May Mr Ellis chose this morning to bless us with his presence. Shortly after 9 a.m. the heavy canoes crossed the bar, and before noon all were aboard. 32 slaves, viz., 19 men, 3 man-boys, 4 women, and 6 girls, and none to be rejected. Delivered up the longboat to Mr Ellis's people, and put the remainder of his bars in her. Her bottom is much eaten with the worm, and I have been much inconvenienced . . .

*

Thursday 6th May . . . Made two trips with the yawl for water and rice. Canoes brought 6 loads of wood. Got on board 4000 lbs of rice, dry and in good order, all hands filled more than 5 butts. Have near 7 tons of rice in good order. One more turn of water and wood in the afternoon finished this troublesome job. Buried a boy slave (No. 189) of a flux. Have a promise, from Mr Ellis, of more trade in the morning if the wind does not suit to sail. Towards midnight wind came off the land with rain.

Friday 7th May Weighed at dawn with the land wind, steered downwards, anchored at 2 p.m. abreast of the trees in 15 fathoms. I think our *Duke of York* has found new heels. All night bad weather; filled 4 casks with rainwater. Passed us in the offing the *Wanderer*.

Saturday 8th May Very unsettled weather with a great deal of rain; could not weigh all day, until 6 p.m. when backed in a hard squall to West. Took the advantage of it and weighed immediately. Turned the yawl off with 3 hands, she being very heavy to tow. We begin to be short of supplies . . .

★

Tuesday 11th May A continual thick fog. At 8 a.m. weighed, run into 11 fathoms which was as near as I dared venture, but could make nothing of the land, though we saw the breakers very high. By noon the wind faint and fog increased. Could not see the land, but by the noise of the surf determined it must be very close. Stood out to 12 fathoms and anchored, for it would not be safe to attempt to steer. Hoisted in the punt and coated her with pitch, tar and brimstone . . .

★

Thursday 13th May . . . We begin to be very short of firewood and water. At noon weighed with the land wind, the fog as thick as ever. Steered upwards by the lead in 13 fathoms. At 3 p.m. anchored, being afraid to keep under sail with us so near in. Propose to try with the boat tomorrow if it does not clear up. Steadfast in my belief that we are close by the factory.

Friday 14th May . . . Mr Smith returned in the afternoon, informed me that we were but a league below the factory. He brought with him fresh water, and the information that they will happily let us purchase 3 tons of rice, of which I am in absolute necessity. Other articles are to be got here without much difficulty. Fired 5 guns while he was away.

★

Wednesday 19th May . . . This morning witnessed the final delivery of 3 canoes of firewood. Have little now to wait here for. Paid with the last of the cloth according to promise. Returned across the bar with the yawl, and prayed a while in the factory chapel. Stood beneath the white-washed walls of the factory, waiting for the yawl to return and carry me back over the bar. Approached by a quiet fellow. Bought 2 strong man-boys, and a proud girl. I believe my trade for this voyage has reached its conclusion.

Thursday 20th May At 2 a.m. weighed with a light breeze at West. Made but little headway because of the great swell. Sounded several times. At dawn buried a man slave (No. 62) who had died of a pleurisy. At noon discovered myself indisposed of a small fever, and my eyes grown very weak. Mr Allen assures me that I am (by God's blessing) sure to recover. The purchase of a relatively modest 210 slaves may yet ensure my continued mortality. In the evening, by the favour of Providence, discovered a conspiracy among the men slaves to rise upon us. Near 30 of them had broke their irons. Secured the men's irons again and punished the ringleaders. Should they have made their attempts upon the coast, when we had a half-dozen out of the ship, I cannot imagine the consequences. They appeared gloomy and sullen, their heads full of mischief. Before midnight buried 3 more women slaves (Nos 71, 104, 109). Know not what they died of, for they have not been properly alive since they first came on board . . .

Friday 21st May . . . During the night a hard wind came on so quick, with heavy rain. Occasioned a lofty sea, of which I was much afraid, for I do not remember ever meeting anything equal to it since using the sea. At dawn brought the ill-humoured slaves upon deck, but the air is so sharp they cannot endure, neither to wash nor to dance. They huddle together, and sing their melancholy lamentations. We have lost sight of Africa . . .

IV

Somewhere in England

1

JUNE 1942

They arrived today. First I heard the distant rumbling of their
trucks, and then the roaring of engines as they laboured up
the hill. I stepped out of the shop and stared. The trucks were
lined up by the gate. A few had already squeezed through and
chipped the gate-posts as they did so. Those that waited kept
their engines running, wasting petrol. Then men began to
tumble from the trucks. They stretched and looked around.
Then, one by one, they began to saunter down the drive.
They looked sad, like little lost boys. Some of the villagers
couldn't contain themselves. They began to whisper to each
other, and they pointed. I suppose we were all shocked, for
we had nothing to prepare us for this. Soon all the trucks
were empty and the last of the men were vanishing down
the drive, nervously smoking their cigarettes, holding them
between finger and thumb. I wanted to warn them, but in no
time at all they were gone. It was too late. We prepared to drift
back to our daily occupations. Mid-afternoon. Summer. The
weather was glorious, and everybody's garden was a riot of
bluebells and daisies. Once the men had vanished, eyes turned
upon me. I was now the object of curiosity. The uninvited
outsider. There was nobody with whom I might whisper. I
stared back at their accusing eyes and then stepped back into
the shop.

JUNE 1939

Every fortnight he came down to town to buy for his shop.
I was the clerk in the warehouse office, charged with keeping
the books right and putting a smile on my face when anyone
came in. And then he came in, but this time with words that
had hitherto been stuck at the back of his throat. He dealt
them carefully. I've been coming in here for some time now.
Yes, I know. You're not wed are you? I shook my head. I was
wondering if you'd care to come out for a drink with me? If I'd
care to? He wasn't much to look at. But he didn't look like he
would hurt. Me, at least. And so I said yes, and found myself
in the snug of the Brown Fox with him and his words. Craftily
dealt, asking me all about myself, interested only – at this stage
– in steering me towards subjects which he no doubt imagined
would make him appear to be a fascinating chap. It made him
a listener and me a talker, but it did not make for fascination.
At some point I told him. I live with my mother, I said. In
1926 she fled to the bosom of Christ. She'd lost her husband,
then she lost her job in the General Strike. Luckily, God took
her up. What I mean is, God took her up to do good works
for Him. On this earth. She hasn't done much since, except
God's work. He nodded and threw me a smile. This man who
in all likelihood had seldom seen the inside of a church. Perhaps
this was what I liked about him. The fact that I could see his
ignorance. Read him like a book. Another drink? Why not?
If he's buying. I thought of my mother. She'll be pretending
she's missing me now. I know her. She'll be looking at the
clock and shaking her head. Wanting to know what I think

I'm playing at stopping out past eight o'clock. Mother, I'm twenty-one years old. She'd perfected a look of such contempt. I got it that night, and for weeks afterwards, whenever I came back from the pub. But she never asked any questions. It was as if she didn't want to ask in case that meant that she cared. That much I understood about her. That she did care, but she didn't want me to know this. She was angry with me. Always angry. He started coming down twice a week. One night, in the Brown Fox, I said yes. But I let him know that I'd rather do it in an office than in a church. I told him that I thought we were both wrong for a church. All that ceremony. What do you think? He agreed, and so I finished my half-pint and made ready to leave. I noticed that these days he didn't spend much time asking me about myself. It was always him now. He told me there were not many lasses up in his village. And being thirty now he'd have to hurry up. He laughed too loudly. As he waited with me by the bus stop, we tried the first experiment of a kiss. I should have known then.

AUGUST 1939

When she realized that I was serious about getting wed to Len she stopped talking to me. I stood before her, but she wouldn't look up. She toyed with her embroidery, passing the antimacassar between her clammy hands, pulling it first one way and then the next. I told her that she would stretch it out of shape, but she wasn't listening to me. She sat impassively, and digested the information that I would soon be gone. She was trying to comprehend the fact that somebody actually wanted me. That in spite of my history I might actually be interesting, if not exactly exciting, to somebody. She'd told me many times that she didn't trust men. They'll just abandon you in the most callous fashion. And hadn't she been right? They're here, and then they're gone. Jesus. Now there was somebody you could trust. When the Lord said come unto me, He didn't mean until the pubs were open, or until He found some other woman. The Lord accepted you with open arms and embraced you. She beckoned me to sit. This house, I thought. I wanted to scream. At least I can get out of this two-up, two-down dump. She put aside her embroidery. Are you sure about this man? Of course I wasn't sure. I'd only known him seven weeks. She looked at me, as though trying to warn me about something. But then, having lost a husband in the Great War, she probably had the right to warn me. I assured her, if there's a war, he'll not be going away. He's got a black lung from being down the pit. If there's a war he's going nowhere. She stared at me. I looked across at my father's picture, which sat on top of the wooden mantelpiece.

I had no memory of him, being just a baby when he died. She had never explained anything to me about this man in a silly felt hat, standing beneath a chestnut tree and staring directly into the lens of the camera. A confident, happy man. A man I feel sure would never have tolerated a woman such as my mother. But perhaps she was different then. Occasionally I've found my dad on a bronze plaque, near the Town Hall, but his name is scattered among the names of hundreds of others. This is merely a place to find him, but not to discover him. When she dies, I'll take it. The photograph might help me to discover him. This is what I think. And then I hear her voice. If you must leave, then do so. I assume that this is her blessing. But she goes on. At least you're not getting wed to a soldier. You should never do that. You'll be left on your own. Then again she's quiet. Just when I'm thinking, that wasn't too bad, she nettles me. Men are at their best in pursuit. I thought I should tell you. But I expect you've found that out already.

JUNE 1942

Apparently we were unlucky to get them in our village. It's all over the papers. We're having an invasion all right, but it's not Jerry. We've been invaded by bloody Yanks. Nobody wants them, but the Hall is large and has plenty of grounds for their tents and things. Everybody expects trouble. People keep talking about their Yank arrogance. Saying that they think that all they have to do is to blow their own trumpets and the walls of Germany will fall down. But our lot are quiet. They keep themselves to themselves, and when they meet us they seem polite. I see them going about their business. And a lot of them like to go to church. They dress so smartly it puts us to shame. The military police are easy to spot with their white helmets and gloves. The truth is, they don't have to mix much with us for they have their own newspapers, films, radio, everything. To most folks' relief, they appear willing to keep themselves to themselves. I met one of them this morning. He was whistling and chewing gum at the same time, which made him look like a fish. When he saw me he lowered his eyes. I could see he was slightly frightened. I said good morning as I passed by, but he shrank a little and pretended not to hear. And then, almost as an afterthought, I heard him whisper, morning ma'am.

JULY 1942

They stand in the shop and talk. Usually two of them.
Sometimes there are three. There is no room for any more.
They tear out their coupons and drop them on to the counter.
I don't care. I've got to ask for them. It's the law. I'm not
playing games. If I go too, who'll look after the shop? They
stand in the shop and talk about the Yanks. They're still
shocked. Upset, even. And then they realize that I'm present,
and that I can hear what they're saying. And so they leave. But
not before they bestow their cigarette-tar smiles upon me. I
heard one of them say, she's missing Len, and I know that I
was meant to hear it.

AUGUST 1942

I'm enjoying the long summer days. I like to watch the sunset
through the pub window. I have my own corner. Well, it's
not my corner, it's just a corner that nobody else seems to
sit in. Maybe nobody else sits in it because they know that
I sit in it. They probably think they might catch something
off a commoner like me. They should be so lucky. Cheeky
monkeys. I don't trouble anybody. I just sit in my corner
and drink my half of bitter and watch the sun set. I didn't
used to do this when he was around. The pub was his place.
Mine was above the shop, waiting for him to come back.
The braggart. I don't think they ever expected to see me
lower myself and come into the pub. I expect they think
I'm lonely or something. Well, they can think what they
like. I'm not looking for anybody. I'm just having a drink.
His best mate is at the bar. He's a crafty bugger. Always
quick to come over, touch his cap, and ask me if I'm all
right. Hardly gives me time to get the words out of my
mouth (I'm all right, Stan, thanks) and he's back at the
bar, foot up, head occasionally swivelling around to look
at me (smile, nod, wink) before he turns back around and
starts talking about me with the rest. I could bloody crown
him. The hypocrite. It's Home Guard this evening. In their
bloody silly uniforms. One gun between them. Whose turn is
it tonight to carry the gun? God help us if this is the best they
can muster up to defeat the Hun. A butcher, a baker, a bleeding
candlestick-maker. Half a dozen farmers and labourers, a
couple of toffs, and a bobby who thinks he's better than the

rest because he's got a proper uniform. He calls the meeting to order. They look at me as though I'm in the way. I stare back at them. We've got to prevent anything from landing in the fields hereabouts. The same conversation as last week. Planes, gliders, airships, 'owt. Airships? I said Airships, all right. Hazards. We've got to put hazards out. Timber, bedsteads, old cars, ranges, anything you can lay your hands on. But that doesn't include the cricket pitch, does it? We don't have to put 'owt on the cricket pitch, do we? It includes the bloody cricket pitch an' all. But that's not right. Bugger what's right, it's what's got to be done. I get up, walk to the bar, and order another glass of beer. Some of them stop listening to the bobby and watch me. The bobby pretends nothing is happening. He continues to talk. It doesn't make any difference that we've got Yanks here now. We've still got our job of work to do, is that clear? They nod. Dogs. He pulls out a piece of paper from his breast pocket. Latest orders for this branch of the Local Defence Volunteers. A chorus of dissent. Home Guard. We've been Home Guard for two bloody years now. Tank traps. We've got to prepare barricades on all roads leading into the village. Broken-down carts, tyres, junk of all kind is to be stationed by the side of the road, ready to be shifted into place. We'll have ditches to dig and we're to stuff them with barbed wire. I'm to carry a gun in case of parachutists. Also, those of you who own motor vehicles, you're to immobilize them when parked. Remove the rotor arm or pull out the ignition leads. There's no chances to be taken, understand? He pauses for a moment, and then scratches his head as though puzzled. I hand the barman elevenpence. Doesn't seem any point to me, says the bobby. Pleasure motoring's forbidden anyhow. Nobody's going anywhere. This is all stuff that they've been doing in the south and other parts for a while now. Seems like they forgot about us. He blinks, takes a swig of beer, and then continues in a more formal voice. But now we've been told, we'll act upon it. Any questions? I laugh as I walk back to my seat, but I manage to get a hand to my mouth. I catch it. Any questions? Sensible questions from this bunch I couldn't imagine. One by one they troop out of the pub. Defeated by their own lack of imagination. I watch the sun go down. And think about Len. Sitting all alone in his cell. I wonder if he's thinking about me. Then I realize that I don't really care. Soon there is only myself, the barman and two of the men in the pub. I close my eyes. Later, I realize that I must have fallen asleep, but they'd chosen to ignore me. I hear one of them whisper, She can't take her drink. If I had twenty-three shillings I'd buy a bottle of whisky. Just to show them. But I don't have it. And then I hear their joke. About the new utility knickers. One Yank and they're off. Their language goes right through me. I pull myself to my feet. Goodnight. Goodnight, I call back.

SEPTEMBER 1939

Our wedding day. Into the Registrar's office. One of the war brides. Get married quickly for now nobody's any idea what's likely to happen. Nobody has. He's got her up the aisle. Nudge, nudge. On my side, my mother. That's all. And on his side, Stan. A couple more mates from the village came down to the big town, but I was barely introduced and they didn't stay. Pathetic, I thought. But then he's got no parents so I shouldn't be so snooty. They'd long since gone. He's only got his mates. I should have been so lucky. I hadn't even got mates. A wedding. My wedding. It was the only wedding I was likely to have, so I thought I'd better do it right. Len was surprised that I didn't have anything in my bottom drawer. Not even a tin of pineapple chunks, or a jar of marmalade. I told him, you're the shopkeeper. My mother, well, she found a way not to cry. Set her face like a mask and just stared straight ahead as if she couldn't see what all the fuss was about. Maybe this reminded her of her day. Maybe she didn't want me to see that she cared. Maybe. Earlier in the month, I'd been with her when the war started. Eleven a.m., Sunday morning. When the National Anthem came on the wireless she stood up. When it finished she sat down and was quiet for a few moments. Then she said that they'd already begun recruiting for Air Raid Wardens. She informed me that this was going to be a civvies' war. I said nothing. She sighed, and then announced that she'd have to start stocking up. She calculated twenty fags at two shillings, tea at two and six, matches a penny ha'penny. She reckoned up how much she could afford to buy with her savings, and I listened. And then I told her that the date was set. A fortnight hence. I'd be wed. But she didn't say anything. She just continued doing her sums in the margin of the previous day's newspaper, using a little stump of pencil that was blunt at one end and chewed at the other.

SEPTEMBER 1939

And then the wedding was over, and we were off to Wales
for a week in a small hotel on Anglesey that seemed populated
with rich ladies who were already hiding from the war. They
always dressed properly, with earrings and lined skirts. They
even dressed for breakfast. Then came their morning walk,
then lunch, gin and tonic, and an afternoon nap. Then cards.
Dinner. Sherry. Bridge. They always stood for the National
Anthem on the wireless come evening. I'm sure they all
harboured a secret desire to salute. The anchor of their lives had
prematurely dropped. I watched them watching me and Len.
All right, so he might not be up to much in your eyes, but he's
decent and honest. Or so I thought. They didn't talk to me.
Sometimes they forgot themselves and nodded as they spread
some jam on their crustless toast. I looked closely. The backs
of their hands were mottled with purple veins. I think they
knew that I was jealous of them. How could they not know?
Why shouldn't I be jealous of them? They had money. They'd
found a way to hide from the world. They had each other. And
there I was. I had Len. I had to train him not to sleep with his
socks on. To undo his shoelaces before he took off his shoes.
To do up his cuffs instead of just rolling them back. He was
thirty going on seven. I liked it when they forgot themselves
and sometimes nodded. But when they saw Len I noticed that
they simply turned away. I wondered what they knew that
they weren't telling me. But I couldn't ask. Len and I were
supposed to be together. A team against the rest of the world.
Man and wife. Him and me. I couldn't side with them.

SEPTEMBER 1939

We got lost on the way back up. Len had borrowed a motor car from one of his farmer friends, but there was only enough petrol to drive us there and back. Petrol had already gone on coupons. We couldn't even go for a spin around Anglesey. So we parked the car up by the hotel and left it. Until we were ready to come back, that is. It was like dusting off an old friend and readying yourself to make an escape. We left early in the afternoon. It's not enough time, Len. Shouldn't we have left earlier? He looked at me. That 'woman, you're talking daft' look of his. Very endearing, I must say. Enough to make you feel like you'd no right to be on this earth. Two hours later, he got lost. Just like I knew he would. It had been a bit touch and go getting down to Wales, but somehow we'd got lucky and made it. Len had pointed out (in his defence) that all the street and road signs had been taken down. In case of invasion. It'll help the Hun. But coming back up our luck ran out. I thought you said you knew the way. I do know the way, I've just got a little mixed up, that's all. A little mixed up seemed to me to be putting it mildly. But there was no point in arguing. No point whatsoever. As the day set around us, we had no idea of where we were. There were slogans in all the papers about saving petrol. They read: Is your journey really necessary? I'd begun to wonder this myself, honeymoon or no honeymoon. Next village, I'll stop and ask somebody, he said. And then I noticed a light on in a small cottage, and Len pulled over. He got out and left me in the car. I saw a woman open the door. They spoke, Len pointed, she looked, I smiled politely. I hated him for doing this to me. Making me feel helpless and at somebody's mercy. Me, I didn't want to be anybody's charity case. Especially not when I was supposed to be with my husband. The man who said that he would protect and honour me. Some joke. Well, Len came back and said we weren't far wrong but we couldn't go anywhere because of the blackout. I said nothing. I just looked at him. I let him know what I thought. And I reckon he understood all right. But he didn't say anything except, come on, let's get our stuff. She's got a spare room and she says that we can have it for the night. Len laughed. Then he went on. I think she's relieved I wasn't the warden. I looked at Len but still said nothing. Reduced to being a bloody beggar. Her husband was already away. Left her and a three-year-old daughter behind. The girl's in bed, she said as she buttered us some bread and asked us if we wanted our eggs turned over. No, mine's fine as it is, said Len, his feet under the table. It's easy to get lost, she assured me. Don't bother, I thought. I already know he's a bloody fool. And then Len did it. He fished into his inside pocket like some bloody spiv. Here, he said. I'd like you to have these. No, we'd like you to have these, he said. We appreciate what you've done for us. And he gave her some coupons like she was a common tart. The look on the woman's face. Well, I nearly died of embarrassment, but I was learning. This was Len. His way of dealing with people. That night I couldn't so much look at him, let alone let him touch me. No, Len. What's the matter? Nothing. Is it because we're in a strange house? Goodnight, Len. I hope this isn't going to become regular. Goodnight, Len. Goodnight, but I'm not right pleased. Goodnight, Len.

SEPTEMBER 1939

When we got back the evacuees had arrived. A dozen boys and girls of a sensible age standing in the church hall. Gas masks in a cardboard box, an identification tag around their necks, and carrying a bundle of personal belongings. They huddled together, their feet swimming in big shoes that were clearly badly scuffed hand-me-downs. Some of them looked as if they had never had a decent meal in their lives. Most of them had already wolfed their emergency rations. A block of chocolate, a tin of corned beef, and a tin of condensed milk. Amongst the grown-ups, confusion and resentment reigned in equal proportion. Why us? None of the other villages had been designated as reception areas. Before us stood a dozen frightened children, the farmers eyeing the husky lads, the girls and scrawny boys close to tears. And then a decision was reached that while it was still light we should send them back. Somebody whispered that all these children wet the bed. That half the mattresses in England were awash, and that at eight and six per child it wasn't really worth it. I looked across at Len, who firmly shook his head. Not even one of them, he said. They can bloody well go back to where they come from. We're not in the charity business. At four o'clock I noticed that the church bells didn't ring. It was a decree. No more church bells because of the war. The children stood in silence.

SEPTEMBER 1942

Today an officer came into the shop wearing dark glasses. He seemed a bit surprised that a bell rang when he opened the door. Excuse me, ma'am. He took his hat off. He should have taken his glasses off as well. I wanted to say to him, it's not sunny out, you know. So you can take them off, you know. Unless you've got something to hide, that is. I've come to talk to you a little about the service men we've got stationed in your village. Oh yes, I thought. It took you nearly three months to get here, did it? Well get on with it then. I'm all ears. A lot of these boys are not used to us treating them as equals, so don't be alarmed by their response. What are they going to do, I thought, throw themselves on the floor before us if we smile? They're not very educated boys and they'll need some time to adjust to your customs and your ways, so I'm just here to request your patience. I see. He relaxes now. Would you like a smoke? No, I don't. Mind if I do? No, go ahead. So he does. Husband out? Yes, he's out, I say. What business is it of yours? I think. Smug bugger. That's what I think of him, standing there in his uniform, telling tales on his fellow soldiers behind their backs. Behind his glasses. Why did you send them to us then? I ask. Why not to some other place? No, no, he says. There's no problem. We're not sending you a problem or anything. It's just that they're different. We want you to know that you'll have to be a little patient, that's all. I smile at him and he smiles back. His white teeth, his confident pose, pulling at his cigarette, lazily blowing out smoke. He really thinks he's something.

NOVEMBER 1942

I stood outside the church today and stared up at the trees. They've worn their leaves shabby. Hardly a breath of wind and they start falling. Ahead of us is winter. And it's not exactly warm up here on this ledge. The wind gets a good go at us and gives us a pounding. Just thinking about it makes me shiver. I turned up my collar and got ready to carry on with my walk. And then I heard their voices starting up. I knew it was them for nobody else in this village sings that way. Like they mean it. I forgot all about the trees and winter. I found myself just staring at the church and listening to the sound of their voices and their clapping hands. Across the road I saw old man Williams. He was out with his dog. He stood and listened as though, like me, he too hadn't heard anything like this before. Just the two of us listening.

DECEMBER 1942

According to today's copy of the *Star*, all over Britain stand-ards of behaviour are breaking down. A young woman Air Raid Warden recently said that if gas spattered her clothes she'd have no hesitation in taking them off and walking starkers. According to this woman, every right-minded person in Britain should be ready to do the same. The *Star* thinks she's barmy. But they don't stop there. It is to be regretted, says the *Star*, that one of the more popular jokes on the factory floor is one which is made at the expense of our boys in the sky. What does an RAF man do when his parachute doesn't open? He brings it back and gets a new one. The *Star* wonders if we're not all the victims of German propaganda that's designed to undermine our confidence. Apparently, some *Star* journalist was outraged because when he was in London he was charged 6d for an apple and a guinea for a pound of grapes. The man who sold them to him then added salt to his wounds by asking him if he'd not heard that there was a war on. I've been getting some choice comments, about tinned sardines and baked beans, for instance. We've had a directive to put up their points value because they've been proving too popular. It's hardly my fault, is it? And as for the National loaf. Well, it's definitely got a khaki tint to it, and it feels to me like paper that's been repulped once too often. Full of straw-like bits. But if you don't like it, nobody's forcing you to eat it. I don't know why they're always complaining to me.

JANUARY 1943

I got a letter from Len. I knew it was him before I opened it. Mean handwriting. And addressed to a Mrs Len somebody. My name isn't bloody Len anybody. Happy 1943! it says at the top. And bits of it are censored. He says that when he comes out he wants us to move away. Further north. Anywhere. But he says that we have to get away from here and start afresh. I see. He claims that he can't stand the shame and he doesn't see why I should have to put up with it too. Well, I'm doing all right. They still talk about me when they think I'm not listening, but I'm doing all right. I don't see why I should have to leave. He'll have to go by himself, I reckon. He can't expect me to follow him around like some silly puppy. No, if he wants to go, then he can go. Good luck to him, I say. I'll have to write to him and tell him this, in a nice way, of course. No need for him to suffer any more than he has to. I've got nothing against Len personally. No reason to hurt him. He just needs to grow up a little bit. A lot. And he'd be better off growing up with somebody else. When I get a minute I'll let him know this. Better he gets it straight. Nothing to be gained by kidding each other. Not now. The best years of our lives and all that. If he wants to sling his hook and go off somewhere, then good luck to him. Good luck to you, Len.

FEBRUARY 1943

Two of them came into the shop this morning. One tall one.
One not so tall one, but he wasn't short either. Far from it.
They were both quite stocky, and both of them were polite.
After all this time, they still seem surprised at how cheap things
are. One woman told me I ought to put up the prices for them.
She said Len would have. I said I know. But look where Len is
now. I didn't tell her this last bit, though. They both took their
caps off. And then they asked me to a dance they're having on
Saturday. Asked me politely. Well, I can't dance, I told them.
You'll learn, said the tall one. He smiled. We've got our own
band, ma'am, said the other one. You hear us play, you can't
help but dance. He laughed. So I laughed too. Then we were
all laughing. A dance, I said. On Saturday, said the tall one.

OCTOBER 1939

Last night I woke up in the middle of the night and thought to myself, bloody hell. What have I done? I've come back to this village with Len, after marriage, after Wales, after being lost. And I'm married now. For nearly a month. A wife. In this bleak and silly little village that's filled with its own self-importance. The only relief I have from this place is when I travel down to see my mother, whose sole occupation in life seems to be to make me feel guilty. A guilt I'm determined to resist. I stare at her as she lies in bed. She's taken to her bed as a permanent place of refuge. I stare at her and listen as she talks incessantly about the phony war. You've been listening to the wireless, haven't you, Mother. She ignores me and continues in her own vein. About how she'll not be digging for victory and growing cabbage and onions. About how, although nothing has happened as yet, they'll soon be coming home in boxes like in the last war. It'll happen, she keeps saying. She pauses, then starts up again. She can't be bothered with her gas mask, she says. All that spitting on the mica window to stop it from steaming up. And it smells, of rubber and disinfectant. I don't tell her that most people have stopped carrying them around. That the novelty has worn off. If you'd have stayed down here you'd have been in Air Raid Precautions, I suppose. WVS, for you. Do you have it up by you? I shake my head. I expect that's why you went, isn't it. Nothing much to do up there except knit socks for the troops. I don't rise to her. Whenever I do she just snaps and tells me not to use Latin in front of her. So I don't bother.

She goes on. But meanwhile, they make us live in the dark like bloody bats. It's ridiculous. Anderson shelter? Two bits of bent steel stuck in the mud, not fit for a pig to wallow in. And nobody'll be hanging out any washing on the Siegfried Line, you mark my words. She knows I'm not really listening to her but she doesn't care. She just likes to have somebody to talk to. Somebody whom she feels it will be all right to bore. She feels she has a right to bore me. I'm her daughter. And then she falls asleep and I have to make my way up the hill on that long, slow bus journey back to the village. It is pretty. I have to give it that. The view from the road, just outside the village, carries all the way across the moors. Well, you'd have to be blind or stupid not to notice that in its own way it's grand. Nothing but green fields and small villages for miles. But then entering our village is like coming into a tunnel. You can't see anything except small houses dotted on either side of the road. And then a big church. A small pub. A nob's hall. Our shop. Some more houses. And so this is my home now. God help me. Maybe I was better off in the warehouse. If I've thought this once I've thought it a million times. But then again, I always say to myself, it's probably just the war. Nothing can look good to anyone in the war. Let's be honest. It's not a great time for anybody. They say that eventually there'll be serious shortages. We'll see.

DECEMBER 1939

I've made a friend. Sandra. She's just had a kid. A boy, Tommy. I don't know if she thought calling him Tommy was funny or something. I've never mentioned it. Her husband has already been called up and gone off. He lives in a photograph on the mantelpiece. There are two leaves to the frame. In the other leaf is a poem:

To My Dear Husband

Where'er you are my Husband true,
In these war-troubled days,
My loving thoughts go out to you
In countless kinds of ways.
God keep you, Dear, where'er you roam,
And bring you, one day, safely home.

That's all that's left of him at present. This picture and when she talks about him. Which she doesn't do all that much. She invited me over for tea. I can see you're a bit lost around here. And Len. Well, he's not the type to go out of his way to introduce you around, now is he. She used to work for Len in the shop. But then she fell pregnant and got wed. I think it was in that order. She offered me a treat. Two Rich Tea biscuits. I expect you have plenty of these in the shop whenever you want them, but for me it's a treat. It's a big thing. Don't get much sweet stuff these days. She sat me down. They say people are queuing in town, trying to beat the system. And that doctors and dentists are hard to come by. Not just panel ones, private too. And that some people are getting mail a week late. I looked at her and wondered if Len had only come after me because he needed somebody to replace her in the shop. Maybe I'm being a bit silly, I thought. Maybe I'm reading too much into everything. I don't know. At least I've made a friend. Sod Len and his pencil-thin moustache. He's happy now that he's got some mug to work for him in the shop. He's happy now that he's able to leave me in the shop and go to the pub with his mates. Are you listening to me, love? Sandra stared at me. You do tend to dream a little, don't you. I've been wondering if I should grow my hair like Veronica Lake. Or if I should just stick to the normal two and sixpenny shampoo and set. I smiled at her. They censor my husband's letters, can you believe that? The kid started to cry. Tommy. Tommy started to play up. She picked it up and held it in her arms. Then she rocked it back and forth until it began to gurgle like it was choking. Tommy's laughing, she said. Here, do you want to hold him? I held up the Rich Tea biscuit. I'd love to, but I've got my hands full at the moment. Got any of your own, have you? Sandra's not much past twenty or so. About my age. I could see that now. Don't look like that, she said. I had to get married and get started. Women in my family go off early. But you've plenty of time yet. Nice of her to say it. Polite of her. She looked sad now. You don't know what it's like when the postman passes the door. The day is ruined. Absolutely ruined. She's the only person I know in the village apart from Len. Long, thin, blonde hair. At first I thought I saw blackened roots, then I realized she was just in some shadow. Why do I have to be so bloody critical? So what if she bleaches her hair? What business is it of mine? I think I'm jealous of her looks. But I do want to be generous to her. Len is a quiet bloke, she says. In his own way he's kind, but it'll take you a while to get to know him properly. Now I resent her. I don't like being told about my own husband. But she feels as though she's helping me. Len hasn't bothered to introduce me to anybody. After all, Sandra has taken it upon herself to come into the shop and find me. A lot of the other girls have gone, she says. There are not many of us left. ATS, munitions work, they've nearly all gone. But some Land Army girls are due to come here. And then there's us. Mothers. I'm not a mother, I say. Sandra smiles. But I suppose working in the shop is vital work, isn't it? They won't put you in the factories, will they? No, I say. I've been classified. Len's disabled. He can't manage by himself, so I'll not be going in the factories. Well, we'll have plenty of time to get to know each other better, then. I'm glad there's somebody around like you. I thought it'd only be me and a few others. And to be honest, most of them are just interested in your business. They're not interested in you, just in what you're up to. I don't have much time for that. Neither do I, I said. Neither do I. She looked at me funny. My mind started to race. I'd been looking right at her. Perhaps she thought I meant her. I couldn't think of anything to say which would convince her that I wasn't talking about her. So I just smiled back. I looked at her with a stupid grin painted on my face. I'm sorry, I said to myself. I don't know how to behave. I like you. I've never been much good with people. She handed Tommy to me. Then she went to fill the kettle again. I knew she was watching me from the kitchen, watching me holding her child, worried that I might do something daft with him. I held him awkwardly. And then I heard the water splashing against the enamel as she started to fill the kettle. But I knew that she was still watching me. I turned around and she beamed at me. Had enough of Tommy? she asked. No. I held Tommy close to me. I'll be all right.

NEW YEAR'S DAY 1940

Len and his mate Stan borrowed a car so they could drive
into town. On business, they said. Drinking business more
like, but I went with them so I could see my mother. I told
them that I'd meet them outside the bank at six. Len didn't
want to see her, but it didn't matter. There was no need for
either of them to pretend. They'd passed that stage. At about
five-thirty, I began to walk back into town, and I noticed that
all the iron railings had been ripped out. By the park. Front
gardens, everywhere. Together with the pots and pans, that
they punctured as soon as you handed them over, the railings
would be used for Spitfires. Things were changing. We'd been
told that in a week or so we'd have to start rationing bacon,
ham, sugar and butter. Customers would only be able to get
them with a ration book. I stood by myself in the cold and
shivered. The moon was full and the sky was bright with
stars. There didn't seem much point to the blackout. I looked
up and wondered if Hitler had found a way to turn out the
stars over his country at night. It was after seven. Len was
late. Bladdered, I imagined. Not for the first time in my life
I felt the humiliation of being abandoned.

MARCH 1940

The cold of winter has insisted on hanging on a few weeks
past its time. Sandra has been looking increasingly lost and
unhappy. These days I go around to visit her two or three
times a week. She can't breast-feed Tommy any more because
she says her milk's all dried up due to worry. He won't take
the bottle, so she has to spoon-feed him, which can take
hours. Tommy has become an increasingly noisy problem,
but I've grown to like him, and to even want to hold him.
I never thought that I would want to hold a baby. Sandra
seems to like this. The fact that I literally take him off her
hands. Today she sat me down and gave me a cup of tea.
And then she told me that she was pregnant. I looked at her
but said nothing. She was expecting me to say something.
That much was clear. She was expecting a reaction of some
kind. Horror. Laughter. Something. But I said nothing. Did
you hear me? I said I think I'm pregnant. No, in fact I know
I'm pregnant. I'm nearly three months gone. She didn't have
to tell me how far gone she was, for I knew that it wasn't
him. I had no idea who it was, but it was clear that she was
hoping that I might ask. But I said nothing. I just sipped
at my tea. A small mouthful at a time. Don't you want
to know who? I was looking out of the window now. As
usual, nothing and nobody in the streets. A perverse part of
me longed for her to tell me that it was Len. But it wasn't.
It's Len's mate, Joyce. Terry. The farmer. She didn't have
to say who Terry was. I wasn't so stupid that I couldn't
figure that out for myself. Sandra's voice began to break.

He gives me extra things for Tommy. Like a baby sister or brother, I said. I couldn't help myself. Do you think it's funny? whispered an incredulous Sandra. She sounded hurt. I was sorry I'd spoken. I apologized. Sandra paused. I don't know what I'm going to do, she said. I'm not going backstreet. I don't want to get rid of it. I'm too frightened to. And I don't want to marry him. Does he want to marry you? I don't know. I don't think so. I hope not, I said. Doesn't seem to me a good enough reason to commit marriage. A bun in the oven. God, she looked pathetic. Helpless. Child in her belly. Tommy in my arms. Cup of tea in her hands. Why didn't she just keep her legs shut? It's easy enough to do. Not exactly difficult, is it? I suppose I was lonely. She answers the question without me having to ask it. I suppose I was lonely and stupid. I should have used something. Yes, I said. Like self-control. Now she was hurt. I could see it on her face. I was sorry I said that. There was a pause and then I continued. I think you'd better write to him. Let him know before he gets back. What do you think? I think so, she says. But what if he doesn't want to come back? What's Tommy going to do for a father? I pointed out the obvious. That this is a war. That if Tommy ends up without a father, he won't be the first and he won't be the last. That's the truth, Sandra. And then she started to cry. I made some enquiries, she said. Her voice quivered. But you can't put it up for adoption without your husband's permission. I'm done for. Dusk approached. The sky got darker. I could see it was freezing out. I would soon have to go and help Len close up the shop. Always a last-minute rush with those coming in from the town. And we've just started to ration meat. I didn't want to leave her on her own in such a state, but what could I do? I touched her arm. Sandra, I said. Write to him. Tell him. It will make you feel better to know that he knows. And they can get leave. Compassionate leave. Then he can come home and the two of you can sort out whatever it is that you've got to sort out. It'll be better that way. I've

not told anybody else, she says. So I'm the only one who
knows? And the doctor. At the clinic in town. It was getting
darker. The shadows were lengthening. I think you should
tell him, I said.

MARCH 1940

Last night Len beat me. After he came back from the pub. Drunk. Once he's got a mood on, that's it. He'll find a reason. It didn't hurt all that much. It happened so quickly. And I understood why he was doing it. Maybe that's why it didn't hurt all that much. He was just working off the embarrassment of not having a uniform. Not even one of the silly bugger Home Guard uniforms. Civvy Street guilt. He was playing at being a man. Secretly drumming on me behind closed doors. But I told him. The next time he raises his hand to me it'll be the last time. Drunk or sober. It'll be the last time.

MAY 1940

France has gone. It looks like we'll have to fight to the bitter
end by ourselves. Everyone's talking of invasion. And what to
do. They say you've got to stay at home. If you're out when
they come, you mustn't run or you'll be machine-gunned from
the air like they did in Holland and Belgium. It says, in the
Star, that you're not to supply the Germans with food, petrol
or maps. And if you see anything at all suspicious you're to go
straight to the police. They sometimes talk to you like you're
mental.

FEBRUARY 1943

I've been thinking about it all week, but trying to pretend that it wasn't a problem. However, this morning I had to face up to the truth. I didn't have anything to wear to the dance. And I simply didn't have the money to go out and buy anything new. A plain dress, some flat shoes and a coat would have to do just nicely, thank you very much. This evening I stood in front of the mirror. When I smiled it took the lines a few moments less to set, and a few moments longer to disappear once I put my face right again. It wasn't my imagination. I didn't have to be told. I pulled on my coat and picked up my handbag, then I walked through the village towards the hall. As I approached, I saw a soldier standing by the chipped gate. Come for the dance, ma'am? I hid my ring. Yes, I've come for the dance. I panicked. Am I the only one? Have I got the time right? He offered me gum. No thank you, I said. I recognized him, I recognized them all from the shop. And they all knew me. I don't suppose they knew my name, but they knew my face. I went inside. There were a few more soldiers in the grounds. Walking around in pairs. Laughing. They seemed odd in this grand place. But then I realized that I probably seemed odd here too. The toffs have moved on for the war. Big of them, I thought. Hey, ma'am. Looking for the dance? I nodded. Over there. He was a military policeman. He pointed with his rifle. I hesitated. Hell, just go straight in. So I did. I walked across the lawn – like a real madam – then up the stairs and into a big room. The first thing that I saw was the food. They had stuff on the table that even I hadn't seen in years. Lemons and grapefruits. Tins of chocolate. Life Savers. Beef steaks. Salami. Sliced tinned peaches. One of them took my coat. May I, he said. Thank you, I said. So polite, I thought. I looked up and saw a few ATS girls from the next village, and some Land Army girls, and a few married ones, all sitting in a line looking frightened. I decided that I'd better go and sit with them. So I went over and sat next to a Land Army girl who was in uniform. She smiled at me but made a point of not saying anything. Then they began to play gramophone records, which didn't make that much sense to me because they were all standing and we were all sitting. What were we supposed to do? In the corner I saw the officer who'd come into the shop and talked to me about them. He looked over and waved. Hello, Duchess. I stared back through him. I was rather proud of this stare. I could see that it upset him somewhat, but he wasn't sure what to do. I kept staring through him. The Land Army girl next to me came to life and wanted to know if everything was all right. I told her, yes, that everything was all right. Why shouldn't it be? I see, said the girl. And still nobody would dance to the gramophone records. And then I noticed that the band were climbing up on to the small stage. They'd pushed some boxes up tight and tacked a cloth drape around the edges, but it looked proper. It looked like a real job, not just something they'd slung together. And then they began to play. It sounded great, but it made everybody feel uneasy. A sitting line of us facing a standing crowd of them. And then I found myself on my feet and walking towards the two who asked me, the tall one and the shorter one. I asked the tall one if he'd like to dance. He smiled at me nervously. I could see the gap in his teeth in the middle of the bottom row. It's usually at the top, I thought. Where people have a gap in their teeth. It's unusual to see somebody with a gap in their teeth at the bottom. But that was all right, it was different and I liked that. He put one hand on my shoulder and held out the other. I stretched my arm out to meet it, and he steered me backwards and into the space that was the dance floor. A foxtrot. Over his shoulder I could see everyone looking on. I could see it on their faces. They were shocked. And maybe a bit jealous, but I didn't care. And then, one by one, the soldiers found the courage to go over to the girls and soon they were all dancing. My partner leant forward and whispered into my ear. Looks like you've started the party. You oughta be proud of yourself. I didn't say anything. You don't seem shy and uneasy like the rest of them. I still didn't say anything. I just listened. Listened to him and listened to the music. You from round here? Why? I asked. Well, I was just wondering. I don't know. I guess you don't act like them in some ways. Can't say how exactly, but just different. Inside I was smiling. That was just what I wanted to hear.

JUNE 1940

Their faces were drawn and defeated. They looked like they'd
seen hell. I couldn't believe that these were our boys, in
shirtsleeves and with no uniforms. Boys is right. That's what
they looked like perched up there on their jeeps and in the
back of the trucks. They were starving. Len and I offered
some of them tea, but they waved their hands and politely
refused. I thought to myself, well, Hitler might as well
just come marching through now. We better start learning
German. Most of them were too ashamed to even look you
in the eye. Our heroes returning from Dunkirk. And yet,
all over the papers, they're still trying to tell us that one
Englishman is worth two Germans, four French, twenty
Arabs, forty Italians, and any number of Indians. I thought,
that fat bastard Churchill will no doubt turn it into some kind
of victory. He'll be on the wireless again tonight, huffing and
puffing, and Len will be lapping it all up like a bloody silly
little spaniel. If Churchill tells me one more time that this war
is being fought for freedom and true principles of democracy
I'll scream. But, as I looked on at them, I thought to myself
that this war can't go on for much longer if this is the state
we're in. That much was clear for anybody to see. It might
as well be the white flag now. We're going to lose England.
We've legally placed ourselves, our property and our services
at the disposal of His Majesty, and I for one don't expect to
get anything back. And sure enough this evening he was on
the wireless, the stuck-up pig. I wanted to turn it off, but Len
likes to listen. So I went out for a walk. One of the LDVs

flashed a torch in my face and asked me who goes there. I wanted to say to the stupid sod, it's me, Hitler. I was hoping you wouldn't catch me because I was planning on invading tonight, starting right here in this village. But now you've buggered up my plans, you crafty devil. Oh, it's just you, Mrs Kitson. I wandered back and sat with Len, who told me that we always start badly. That we English lose every battle but the last. He'd believed the official story behind the looks on those lads' faces. I was getting good at learning the difference between the official stories and the evidence before my eyes. And even when there was no evidence, I was learning what to disbelieve. And so I sat with Len and began to swear out loud. What's the matter with you? Nothing, Len. Nothing. I'm just fine.

MARCH 1943

I've been wondering about him ever since the dance. I didn't
think he was letting me down by not showing up at the shop.
I'm not that presumptuous. After all, we only danced a few
times and then I was passed around. It was only fair. There
wasn't enough of us so we had to be shared. It turned into a
'Ladies, excuse me' dance, which meant anyone could cut in.
At the end of the dance we all left together, so there was no
question of anyone walking out with anyone. They brought
us our coats, and gave us presents. An orange, a pack of
cigarettes, and some candy, as they call it. Chocolate is what
we call it, and for most of us it was like being given lumps
of gold. The Yanks really have no idea of what it means. I
think we were maybe a bit rude, like kids, for once they'd
given us the chocolate we all muttered a hasty goodnight.
Everyone just wanted to escape with the chocolate in case
the Yanks changed their minds. The next morning I woke
up and thought about him. I wondered if they'd be having
another dance for us, or if they'd decided that one was enough.
I decided that all dances should start that way, with me and him
gliding across the floor and breaking the atmosphere. That was
three weeks ago. I have a feeling that they thought me a bit
above myself. But still, I have nice, if awkward, memories.
But today everything is fine again, for he came into the shop
with a big smile upon his face and a bunch of daffodils. He
told me that he didn't know what we called these things. He'd
never seen them before, for they didn't have them where he
came from. But he thought he'd like me to have them. He

dresses so smartly, and he doesn't chew gum when he talks. Not like the officers and the others. I don't know why they think it's so clever to do this. It's vulgar. Anybody could tell them that. His hair is well combed, with a sort of razor parting on the left. It's short, like thin black wool, but he puts some oil or something on it because it shines in the light. Quite bright, actually. Here, take them. He handed the flowers to me and I thanked him. I looked for a jam jar to put them into and he lit a cigarette. Excuse me, do you mind? he asked. Of course I don't mind. I don't say this, but I hope he understands. I just shook my head a few times. I'll be back in a sec, I said. You don't mind watching the shop, do you? I went out the back and found a jar. I wondered if I should ask him. I didn't know why I was even going through this for it seemed obvious to me that if I didn't ask him then nothing was going to happen. I took a peek back through into the shop and saw him just standing there like a spare part, not knowing what to do. And then I came back in with the daffodils standing proudly in a jar. I just asked him outright. Would you like to go for a walk? He looked confused. As though I was trying to trick him into something. A walk? Or perhaps you're not allowed to do this. To go off limits, or whatever you call it. Is that it? If so, I'm sorry for asking, but it's just that I thought a walk would be nice. Still, it doesn't matter if you're not able to do it. No, he says. But maybe Sunday. I don't think we get any recreation again until Sunday. Would that be all right? We get most of the day. I looked at him and realized that Sunday it would have to be. We sometimes go to your pub. It seems a nice place. Most of the guys like the English pub, although your beer still tastes a little strange to us. But you do like it? I asked quickly. Yeah sure, we like it. We drink it. There's nothing else to drink. He laughed as he said this. I don't mean to be rude, he assured me. Look. I've got to get back. I've got duties to take care of. Sunday, I said. Sunday, he said. And that was him gone, leaving me with the daffodils.

JUNE 1940

I can't figure out if Len is trying to impress me by joining the Local Defence Volunteers (or Look, Duck, Vanish, as people call them – they even call themselves this). Or maybe Dunkirk has secretly shaken him up. An army instructor came to one of their meetings in the pub. Taught them the German for 'Hands up!' Showed them how to spot different types of aircraft, how to handle a rifle and bayonet. Last Sunday, he took them out into the woods and they used grass sods as grenades. They're planning campaigns. Making decisions. Do we march east to protect Sam Smith's brewery, or north to guard Joshua Tetley's brewery? But Len is getting bored. He's younger than most of them. I think it's making him feel guilty. Reminding him that he should be in the real army. He'll soon stop going. LDV service is compulsory, but nobody really bothers that much by us. There isn't really anyone to check up. We're off the beaten track. They're more bothered by those dodging proper military service. Len's black lung is an embarrassment to him, but it's a genuine handicap. He's better than some of his mates, who are skiving off with all kinds of made-up illnesses and ailments. Now they've got something to be embarrassed about, not Len.

JUNE 1940

I was serving two Land Army girls. We all heard the shot. I
ran straight from the shop up the street, hair flying this way,
legs that. I knew she wouldn't tell him. Straight into the house
and there she was, lying on the floor, blood spreading. And
Tommy screaming. And that bullying bastard sitting there as
bold as brass with the rifle in his hands and tears running down
his cheeks. He kept repeating himself. Get the police, I've just
done in my missus. The dirty bitch. Sandra had her eyes open
and was staring into mid-air as if nothing was the matter. I've
just done in my missus. The dirty bitch. As if she couldn't
quite understand what all the fuss was about. The thing I
noticed about him, though, was his uniform. It seemed odd
that he should be sitting there in his uniform. Back from the
war to kill. His wife. I told her to write the bloody letter,
but she would have to do it her way, wouldn't she. And look
where it landed her. Somebody must have already called for
the coppers, because it didn't take them long to arrive. When
they did, he just got up and went with them. One of the
coppers put a blanket over Sandra, like she was asleep. Then
he told me that there was no point in my sticking around.
I might as well get along, hadn't I. He offered to escort me
(his words) out of the house. Somebody had already taken
Tommy.

JUNE 1940

Tonight I saw Len, sitting in the pub with his mate, Terry the Farmer. Len was always lecturing me. You don't mix with anybody. It's all right, you know. You can come into the pub for a drink with us. We won't harm you. How do you expect anyone to get to know you if you won't show your face out? I'd generally look at him, but say nothing. And off he would go to the pub and leave me sitting by myself, listening to ITMA on the wireless. But tonight I went to the pub. I put on my coat and walked up the road. He was sitting in the corner with the man Sandra's husband should have shot. Mr bloody Farmer perched there like Lord Muck, everybody knowing it was him who'd done it to her, sipping a pint like nothing was the matter. What'll you have? asked Len. I'll be having nothing, I said back to him. Nothing as long as you're sitting here with this slack bastard. I could see it in Len's eyes that he was ready to belt me one there and then, in front of everybody. If he wasn't so vain, he'd have done it. I think you'd better go home, was the best he could come up with. Why? I asked. Because I said you'd better. So I turned and left. I didn't have any desire to argue with him. And I didn't want to sit in the same place as him as long as he was with that bastard. So I turned and walked back out and into the night. It was so quiet. It was like the whole world had stopped because of this bloody stupid war. And what about Tommy? I supposed they'd find a good home for him. I walked back to the shop, went upstairs, took off my clothes, and climbed into bed. I didn't want Len near me. Not now, not ever. And I didn't want him to see me crying.

JULY 1940

All I could think of this morning was that a whole month has passed since Sandra died. And then the inspector showed up. I was standing in the shop with Len, going through the books for the week, when suddenly we heard a van pull up. Len went to the window and fingered the curtains. Then he turned to me and shouted in a whisper that I'd got to go out the back with the eggs and get rid of them. I didn't need telling twice. He doesn't tell me much, doesn't Len, but I wasn't born yesterday. I work in the shop with him. I'm married to him. I know his game. I dashed into the back of the shop and started to push everything into a flour sack. Hurry up, you silly cow. Why should I hurry up if this is the best he can call me? I heard the doorbell ring, and then there were voices. Me, I took the sack and went out the back. Then I was away through the woods and down the hill, laughing all the way like a crazy bugger. When I got to the stream, I opened the sack up wide. There was nobody around. I was standing by myself. That bastard Len. I knew it was a crime. It was madness. It was the sort of thing that somebody who was plain bloody daft would do. I knew all of this. But I did it anyway. I just threw everything into the stream. Egg after egg. Let the fish or whatever have them. Len said to get rid, so I was getting rid. I'd just pretend that I didn't understand what he meant. I thought, it's a hell of an expensive way to spite somebody, but he bleeding well deserves to be treated with spite. When I'd finished, I sat on the bank and laughed. I didn't know what the bloody hell I was doing in this place. With him. I couldn't be any worse off

172

in a factory or in the WAAF. I must have been mad. It was mad. To have come to this place at all. I picked up the empty flour sack. Then I looked at the stream. I threw the sack in after the eggs. I didn't want any of it. What did I need with an empty sack? I didn't want any of it. By the time I got back from the stream he was in the pub. It was night. I was asleep when he came in. Or at least I was pretending to be. He asked me, so I told him that I'd done what he wanted me to do. I'd got rid of them. He laughed. Then he reminded me that tea and margarine were now on coupons. Then he went to the bathroom. When he found out that it was the truth that I'd told him, I knew he'd want to take a strap to me. But until then he laughed. I think he liked me for a minute or so. He thought I was funny.

SEPTEMBER 1940

Apparently, London is still getting it bad. It's their turn every night. I've been reading about it. It's all in the papers. ARPs can get no sleep. They're working hand in hand with the police force around the clock. UXB means unexploded bomb. They say if a bomb's got your name on it, you hear a whine, then a silence before the explosion. This is because it's travelling faster than sound. Those who've dug in their shelters stand a better chance. There's those that will take your bolts, spanners and sheets, and put your Anderson into the ground for you. But it will cost you a few bob. There's money to be made out of misery. Torches, batteries, firemen's axes, chemical fire extinguishers, whistles, you name it. You can even buy ARP-approved bomb removers. Top of the line is 'The Gripper' – 'grips bombs from any position only 10/6'. If it got a bit lively outside, I'm not sure if I'd want to get into a shelter. They say you've to take food, warm clothing and blankets to make yourself as comfortable as possible, and sing songs like 'Me and My Girl' and 'Swanee River'. It doesn't sound like me. Today Len caught me reading the papers. He asked me why I'm always reading, reading, reading. I didn't say anything. Then he said we might lose the war. He reckons being up here, we don't really understand how bad it is. We get a rosier picture. The war's still a bit of a joke to us. I thought, he's changed his tune. But I said nothing. The *Star* has started to run a competition called Hitler-Hits. They give you the first line and whoever sends in the best second line gets £10.

If you listen in Hamburg you may hear Lord Haw-Haw say,
We've killed 10,000 Englishmen – one less than yesterday.

I wish I'd have thought of that one. Today's first line is a
hard one,

On every hand in Germany it's very plain to see . . .

NOVEMBER 1940

That silly brummie bugger Chamberlain's dead. Almost exactly six months after stepping down. Common opinion is that the strain of holding the highest office killed him. Our blackout curtains need to be fixed. The bobby told Len that last night he saw light. I went into my sewing box to find a needle and thread. I thought, they're a blessed nuisance. The curtains, that is. Then I saw a rag doll I'd been making for Tommy out of old stockings. I'd only to sew on the buttons for eyes. That was all I had left to do.

DECEMBER 1940

Thursday was always a popular going-out night in town. I wonder if Hitler knew this. Maybe it was simpler than this, maybe he just knew it was going to be a full moon. It was the clearest night I'd ever seen. I could hear the town sirens in the far distance, wailing their warning, and then I heard the queer engines of German bombers, all out of tune. They sounded different from ours, uglier. And then, away on the horizon, our boys; the ripping sound of anti-aircraft batteries. Everybody knew they were after the steelworks. Firth Brown and Co., J. Arthur Balfour and Co., Vickers. All of them. But there were too many Jerry planes and I knew we were going to get a pasting. It was a real bomber's moon, and from up there in the sky our roads must have looked like frosty white ribbons pointing the way to the target. First flares, then incendiaries, then the heavy bombs. We all stood shivering on the hillside and looked down. The town soon looked like a thousand camp fires had been lit on it, beautiful little fairy lights, everywhere blazing. You couldn't look anywhere without seeing fire. Len slipped a blanket around my shoulders, and the vicar started singing 'Nearer my God to Thee'. I gave him a dirty look, but he didn't stop. In between the verses, I heard somebody whisper, The town's on fire. There was a huge celestial glow, as though the sun were about to rise out of the heart of the town. And then the vicar stopped. He pulled a piece of paper from his frock pocket and announced, 'Repose.' There were maybe two dozen of us. We all turned from the town and looked at him.

God is our Refuge – don't be afraid,
He will be with you, all through the raid;
When bombs are falling and danger is near,
He will be with you until the 'All Clear'.
When the danger is over, and ev'rything calm,
Thank you Redeemer for courage and balm;
He'll never forsake you, He'll banish your fear,
Just trust and accept Him, and feel He is near.

When he finished, there was silence. We all turned and looked back at the town. Fires were still blazing, but we couldn't hear any more planes. Maybe it was over? Len whispered in my ear, I'm off to the pub. I'll see you back later. I watched him and his mates walk off. I even heard them laughing. I imagined that I could hear the sound of the 'All Clear' in the distance. But, of course, I heard nothing. And then I looked around at the vicar who was praying, stifling his fear between two folded hands.

DECEMBER 1940

Today I took a bus down to the town to find my mother. I hadn't slept much. In fact, I hadn't really slept at all, but I felt wide awake. The countryside looked much the same, but when I saw the town, I wanted to cry. Tram lines were twisted like liquorice. Iron girders were discarded across the street, jutting up into the air and pointing towards the now empty gray sky. I couldn't believe that this was my town. The bus couldn't go any further, so we all got off and began to walk. I stared at buildings that were now reduced to one or maybe two walls. Neat rectangular holes that used to be windows provided useless ventilation. Everywhere I looked I could see mountains of rubble, crushed cars, and battered trams. Up above me, the loose, swinging arms of cranes picked their way over the carcass of the town. And in the streets, men with flatcaps and women with head-scarves scavenged at the ruins of their houses, avoiding any hot debris, trying to find bits of furniture, photographs, anything that remained of their lives. As they did so, others – maybe family members – stared on, dumbstruck. I stepped gingerly around a sea of broken glass, and then saw a formal queue of parents taking turns to lift their children into the cockpit of a crashed Jerry bomber. I wondered about the pilot, and then realized that I should be wondering about my mother. I increased my pace. Down a side street, I saw charred bodies covered in soot and glass. Then I realized that they were just Burton's dummies. It occurred to me that I was lost. That all the familiar landmarks had gone and that I was no better than the sad woman I saw wandering with a bird cage in one hand and some photographs in the other, singing 'It's a long way to Tipperary'. The bashing had obviously sent her beyond. I asked for directions from an ARP who looked half-asleep underneath his tin helmet. He said nothing, but simply pointed me towards a junction that I recognized. I wanted to ask him about the football rattle in his hand, but he looked too tired to answer, so I just said thank you. He nodded a quick acknowledgement. I walked on knowing that there was no longer any such thing as a familiar route. Fire hoses like long, endless snakes were strewn across the roads. Fires still spat, but down here the odd girder was all that remained of most buildings. I saw groups of patient employees standing outside shops and offices with no idea of what to do, their work places wrecked. The whole town was in a state of shock. Everybody seemed to be suffering their own private war tragedy. The odd car rolled by at a funereal pace, but heads didn't turn. People simply gawked at the destruction. I turned off the main street and continued to pick my way through the back streets. I looked on at the ATS girls, who seemed to be working non-stop, helping the police, driving, standing side by side with the ARPs. They made me feel useless.

DECEMBER 1940

I suppose I knew that she'd be dead before I got there. It didn't seem possible that others should have died, but not her. I saw the house, or what was left of it. A gap in the street, like a broken tooth. There were no windows, the front door hung off its hinges, and I could see that the ceiling plaster was down and that soot and dirt were everywhere. Nothing looked burned, so I knew that it wasn't an incendiary. These could be put out with earth and water. That much I'd managed to understand from the papers, not that she would have bothered to do anything about it. It looked like the blast had come from a nearby bomb. And then I saw that the houses across the road had been hit. The ARPs were still cordoning off the road. I saw old Mr Miles. On his back he had a leather coat so mangled it looked like someone had thrown a dead cow over him. When he saw me, he handed his roll of string to another warden. I ducked under the barrier. He put his hand on my shoulder. I'm sorry, love. He took off his tin helmet. You know what she was like. She wouldn't go in the shelter. She made us laugh, though. She said, I've never had a front seat in a war, and I'm not missing my chance now. Where is she? I asked. They've taken her off in a corporation bus with the others. It were not good around here as a lot of folk took their chances. They weren't banking on a direct hit. If you're a bit squirmish, you'd best make yourself scarce. We're not finished yet, and there's more trapped under that lot. I looked behind him as his fellow men, cigarettes dangling from their lower lips, feet stamping to keep themselves warm, shovels in

181

hand, prepared to dig again in the rubble. You'll get a chance to see her later, love. They'll not be burying anyone for a while. Can't do nothing for them. I expect they'll want you to give identification. And don't worry about your household salvage. There'll be no looting while we're about. So don't worry. You can come back later today, or tomorrow. Sort out your stuff. I looked into Mr Miles's tired and crease-lined face, and I knew that this kind old man was near the end of his tether. I wondered how many others he'd had to talk to like this.

DECEMBER 1940

By mid-afternoon it had started to snow. I was sitting in the park watching the endless flow of people filling tin baths from the lake. There was no water. After Mr Miles had sent me on my way, I spent a couple of hours wandering around the town in a daze. I'd noticed the long queues at standpipes. In some lucky streets, the water cart arrived with its large round cylinders. People with buckets and jugs and saucepans, whatever they had, pushed and shoved. The water, flecked with charcoal and lime, spluttered out of large taps, but at least you could drink it. And then the water-cart man shut off the taps and there was no more. That's it until tomorrow, loves. And off he went to another lucky street. Some went back to the standpipes. I continued to walk and saw folk rummaging like paupers among the rubble of their houses. I spied on people's lives. The fronts of their houses were often blown clean off, leaving the furniture still arranged, books and crockery in place. In one house, a hole in the back of a cabinet, that must have been previously hidden against a wall, was now revealed for all to see. Nearly everybody's roofing slates had slid down and into the street, exposing sad, gaping lattice work. Some had been really unlucky. The insides of their houses had collapsed, mixing brick, wood and glass with papers, curtains and clothes. Ladders were up against what walls remained, and broken furniture was stacked neatly on the pavement. I couldn't stand it any more. The Church Army Mobile Canteens, the WVS Mobile Canteens, the Salvation Army Mobile Canteens, all bringing food and drink to the workers and the homeless. In one street, Jerry had dropped a thousand-pounder bang in the middle of the tram track. The overhead wires were all down. A little girl was bawling as she looked at the burned-out shell of the tram. And outside a barber's shop, a sign: 'We've had a close shave. Come and get one yourself.' I walked on in my dazed state, trying not to think of her lying wherever she was. And then I went into the park where I must have fallen asleep. The snow woke me up, cold flakes slapping against my cheeks. I opened my eyes and peered through the pale, watery light of afternoon. It was then that I saw people filling tin baths from the lake. I decided to go back to the village. There was no point in going back to the house and sorting through her things. They'd be wet and useless. And no point in going to find her. She didn't need me at this moment. I decided to get back to Len. To get back to the village.

DECEMBER 1940

The corporation buried them today. Christmas Eve. Some had
private services, but most went at the same time. They were
all there, the dignitaries. The Lord Mayor, representatives of
the Civil Defence Services, clergy from all denominations. I
stood in the snow. It had snowed for nearly two weeks now.
I thought of her standing looking up at the skies as Jerry
dropped his bombs. The best cinema show in the world. I
imagined that's how it must have looked to her. Standing out
there in the cold night air, with all that noise, and the red glow
of the fires lighting up her neighbourhood. I could picture the
child-like pleasure on her face. And then the service was over
and we began to leave the cemetery. I remember thinking that
it didn't feel like Christmas. And that it was so cold that I
would have to ask the fuel controller for extra coal.

JANUARY 1941

I read in the *Star* that the King and Queen visited the town yesterday. They stayed three hours and visited bombed-out houses and talked to folk. All I could think about was the smell of the chemical lavatories and cesspools in people's back gardens. I hope the corporation did something about them. There's nothing anybody can do about the snow. It's not stopped for weeks.

FEBRUARY 1941

Len, of course, had refused to come to the funeral. She never did like me, he said. But that wasn't the point. As far as I was concerned, it was a matter of respect. Who said that she had to like you? She tolerated you. That was a lot for her. Believe me. But Len still wouldn't come to the funeral. When I got back from the funeral he laughed at me. He lowered his newspaper. She died because you left her down there on her own and went off with me, he said. I walked out of the room. I decided that on the first Sunday of every month I would take the bus into town. I would play daughter. This morning was Sunday. Despite the cold I had no choice. There's one bus in the morning and one that comes back at night. They've cut to a skeleton schedule, having decided to commandeer the buses to serve as emergency ambulances. This being the case, I knew right off that I would have to spend the whole day there. It didn't take long at the graveside. It was very much a matter of Hello, Mother, how are you? Hope you've found Dad again. And if you've found him I hope you're happy. Happier than I 'am, at any rate. I can't rightly see how you couldn't be. You'd have to be a miserable bugger to be unhappier than I am. Now that she was with her maker I had the feeling that she was listening to me. Which is more than she ever did when she had some breath in her body. I left, then decided that I should buy her some flowers. I bought them at the hospital next door. Handy that, having a hospital right next door. I suppose some might look upon it as being a bit creepy, but I didn't think so. After I'd bought the flowers I walked back into the cemetery and laid them on the grave. I stood back. I wondered if it was possible to place them in such a way that people would understand that they were meant for my mother and not for the other two people who shared this communal grave with her. An infant. Didn't last a day. Its mother had no money. Probably no bloke either. And an old man. Truly old. Lived sadly past his time until there was nobody left. Probably wore out his memories like a gramophone record that's been played too often. I tried to place the flowers so that Mother would know. But did it really matter? After all, nobody had brought flowers for the other two. Let them all share them, I thought. And then I went for a walk in the park. I sat by the lake and stared unashamedly into space for the rest of the afternoon. People used to come and feed the ducks. But nobody's got bread to spare any more. The ducks have to eat whatever it is they used to eat before people were generous. Then the weather turned bad again. It began to snow. The branches of the trees were already bowed under a thick crust of ice. So I went to the pictures to get out of the cold. I found it difficult to find a cinema without a House Full sign. Other people must have had the same idea before me. Lonely people. Single people have no shame about going to the cinema. Why should they? It's dark. Nobody can see them. Nobody cares. But these days, I hate the films. Short government instructional films on how to win the war. They treat you like a fool. What to do. How to do it. How to save. What to save. And then a feature about how classless England is now that we're all pulling together to win the war. Classless my arse. A toffee-nosed bugger's still a toffee-nosed bugger to me. And then the lights came on and we all filed out. Outside it was getting a bit dark. I waited at the bus stop. There were a few people I recognized in the queue. They nodded, then wrapped up warm and kept themselves to themselves. Like me, they're likely to have been visiting family or friends. Except in their case I imagined their lot were still alive. The bus takes about an hour or so to reach the village. Longer these days. As we laboured up the hill, the tyres spat gravel and ice behind them. We're its last but one stop. We clambered off and tried to avoid giving each other a final nod. And we succeeded quite well. Very well, in fact.

JULY 1936

Everyone at the factory's going off for the summer. Most of them are going to Scarborough, but some are travelling across the way to Blackpool. They've all got a real beano in mind. But me, well, I'll not be going anywhere. I know that she won't let me. She'll just tell me it's a waste of money and that will be the end of it. There won't be any discussion, that will be it. Like when she made me leave school four years ago. I told her that Dad would have wanted me to get my school certificate, and maybe even one day go to college. She just stared at me and said, How do you know? She spoke to me as if he were nothing to do with me. I didn't say anything else. As a child, I soon learned that it was best to say as little as possible to her. But whenever I picked up a book to read she would finger her Bible and look askance at me. She once hit me because she said I read too much. Apparently, there was no need to read so much. It was wilful disobedience on my part. She didn't seem to understand that this was my way of hiding from her. Everything was seen as some kind of betrayal of her. I was always a disappointment. So I had to leave school and go to work. After all, I couldn't expect her to support me any longer. How did I imagine she'd managed up until now? And so I left school. I've learned, over the last four years, to ignore her. To try not to hear her bleating, self-important voice. And I've continued to lock myself up in books. And now everyone's talking about going off for the summer. But they haven't asked me to go with them. They haven't even asked me if I'm going somewhere else. They're not interested.

I expect they imagine they'll get the same frightened answer that they got when they once asked me to a dance. I'm sorry, I stuttered. I expect they think I'm coy because I'm not much to look at. She doesn't go anywhere because she's ugly. Well, it's true, but it's not the whole story. It's not even the half of it. I'm just happier with books. They don't shout at me, or accuse me of anything. They don't even know that I'm not much to look at.

CHRISTMAS 1936

I've got an extra job tearing tickets at the Lyceum Theatre ('Yorkshire shows for Yorkshire folk'). Something to keep me out of her house for a bit longer each day. Once people are in, I get to see the show. But it's not much of a show. In fact, it's the pantomime, Mother Goose, but at least I'm getting to know a new world, and meeting people from a different background. That's how I met Herbert. He's an actor. He talks to me about Shakespeare. He seemed surprised that I'd read some of Shakespeare's plays, and some poets like Wordsworth and Coleridge and so on. Herbert has begun explaining to me about the difference between comedy and tragedy. We talk a lot about these things. He laughed when I told him I hated my name because there were no Shakespearean characters called Joyce. We usually have a drink before the show. He's trying to get me to like gin. I'm always trying to get the glass back on to its wet spot on the bar. And then, last night, Christmas Eve, I agreed to go out with him and the rest of the cast after the play had finished. There's always places that will stay open for actors. Everybody seems to love actors. We all toasted Christmas as the clock struck twelve. Then later, having walked me home, Herbert kissed me goodnight outside the house and said how much he loved me. All I could think of to say was, I'm eighteen. He just smiled and kissed me again.

APRIL 1937

She didn't even knock. She just came straight into my room and stood waiting for me to say something to her. I couldn't say anything because I couldn't stop crying. It annoyed me that she refused to see this. That she wouldn't even acknowledge the fact that I was really upset. He wasn't replying to any of my letters. None of them. And there was nobody at the factory that I could tell. She took a long look at me, but all she could say was, It's the first time in ages I've seen you without a book. And I thought about it. She was right. But she didn't even ask me why I was crying. If she had have done, I would have told her. But it was as if she just wanted to see what the noise was all about. And once she'd found out, she left and closed the door behind her.

MAY 1937

After the abortion, I went to church with her. Or, as she put it, I came to Christ. I still worked at the factory, but I said even less than before. I didn't talk to anybody at all, even if they spoke to me. It was part of my performance. I didn't speak. But I thought that Christ might be prepared to speak with me. At least He might express some interest in me. But He didn't. So I left the church. Or I left Christ. I could never figure out which. And then she left me. My abandonment of Christ was the last straw. I'd chosen to leave He who had made her life possible. This was, for her, the unkindest cut of all.

CHRISTMAS 1937

On the train down, I stared out of the window. I would be spending every penny I'd ever managed to save in my life. When I got to London, I moved into a bed and breakfast near King's Cross station. It occurred to me that I could last – with some luck – perhaps a lot of luck – four days. And then I didn't know what. I found Herbert on the second day. He was at the Lyric Theatre playing in Mother Goose. A different production. Even though it was London, it seemed a worse production somehow. Even the posters were shabby. The whole thing was disappointing. But not as disappointing as Herbert, who got me a seat in the stalls and said we could talk afterwards. In a pub in Hammersmith that was thick with tobacco smoke. The Dog and Pheasant. He bought me a gin, and a pint for himself. And then he said he couldn't reply to my letters. He told me about his wife and his two children, and I listened with my mouth open. And then I spilt my drink. It toppled over and I watched as it pooled on the table. He bought me another gin, then said he had to get some Woodbines from the bar. I never saw him again. I sat there by myself, an idle finger spinning the ice. I'd been jilted. I realized that Herbert had no idea of what it was like to be anyone but himself. But this didn't make any sense, because he was supposed to be an actor. And then it was ten o'clock and I heard the landlord shouting. Time, ladies and gentlemen, please. Let's be having you. Time. Outside the pub, a man asked me if I had a light. Then, before I could answer, he winked at me and smiled. He had yellow teeth. My stomach turned a slow somersault.

FEBRUARY 1938

This morning I started a new job. In a warehouse which imports foodstuffs from all over the country and abroad. My job is to serve the people who come in. Shopkeepers, mainly, from all over. I'm supposed to look cheerful. And talk. The factory. Well, they'd had enough of me not saying anything. But I hate this new talking job. I hate this town. I'm trying to start reading again, but it's not easy. Every night I hear the dull beat of her feet as she drags herself up the creaking stairs. Then I realize that I'm no longer sure of why I'm reading, let alone what it is that I'm reading. I just want to cry, but I've promised myself that I'll never let her see me cry again. Never.

SEPTEMBER 1941

It's autumn. I've been here two years now. I've resigned myself to the fact that I won't ever like it. But at least I don't pretend. Len knows how I feel. He also knows how I feel about the war. I hate the 'Wings for Victory' and 'Salute the Soldiers' weeks. I'm just waiting for it all to end and then I'll be off. Today I asked Len about his parents. He's usually reluctant to talk about them, but for some reason he rested down his cup on the kitchen table and began to speak. But he didn't look me in the eyes as he did so. He talked for a good while, in fact until I thought he might cry. But he didn't. He was quiet for a while, and then he simply stood up and went out. I knew then that we'd never really been married. We didn't know each other. We didn't trust each other. Later on, he came in drunk and talking nonsense. He told me that he thought Hitler looked like a hysterical lavatory brush. And that because Russia was the only country to stand up to Hitler, maybe their system was right. I expect he heard this rubbish in the pub. He slumped against me as I helped him up the stairs to bed.

DECEMBER 1941

Len's in prison for doing what hundreds of others, the length and breadth of this country, are still doing. Namely, trading in the so-called 'black market'. They took him away the day after the Americans were gracious enough to join us in the war. The fact that they chose to stand by and watch as we lost Norway, Belgium, France, Denmark and Holland only served to stir up plenty of negative passions towards them. I sat with Len and listened to the announcement on the wireless. When it was over he snapped the *Star* shut and dropped it by the side of the armchair. Then he stood up. I heard the door slam, and his boots register on the cobbles. And the next morning the inspectors arrived. Representatives of the Price Regulation Committee of the North East Region, based in Leeds. To pinch him. But Len had gone to town. He had been warned three times, but he wouldn't listen. Eggs could be bought only for the purposes of hatching, but farmers, shopkeepers and customers formed a partnership that made a nonsense of such decrees. Only Len would have to pursue his subversive activities on a grand scale. One thousand eggs. Possibly more. Officially, you could only charge 3¾d for an egg. But there were plenty who'd pay up to 15 shillings for a dozen. Len was well aware of this. They waited outside in the motor car until Len came back up from town. When he did, he knew straight away that something was up. They followed him in the door. The two of them. Len looked at me, and then back at them. He spoke to them like he was talking to a pair of hounds. You two. What do you want in my shop? It's

198

you we want, lad, they said. We've found what we're looking
for. And we've got your mate. Now you'll be coming with us.
Len spun around and stared at me. What have you told them?
I shrugged my shoulders. You didn't tell them 'owt, did you?
The inspectors looked at him. Is there something she shouldn't
have told us, is that it? Course not, snapped Len. You're a
lying bastard, aren't you. Len moved towards me. One of
the inspectors put his hand on Len's arm. All right. You're
coming with us, and the door's this way. Your wife can bring
your things along later. No need for you to get alarmed now.
It's all pretty straightforward. You arresting me? We're taking
you in, lad. I told you. We've already got your farmer mate.
The two of you will have plenty of time to get your story
straight. What about her? Are you suggesting we take your
wife as well? Len glared at me as though I were somehow
responsible. But he couldn't say anything, otherwise it would
look as though he was guilty of something. Which, of course,
he was. So he allowed himself to be marched off in silence.
And I slept well that night. I stretched out in the bed. I knew
that whatever happened, I wouldn't have to share my bed with
him again. That if he came back now, I'd stand up all night in
the corner of the room before I'd ever condescend to join him
in bed. Something was lifted from me the moment they took
him away. My chest unknotted. I could breathe again. He
expected and received little sympathy from the Magistrate,
who terminated his speech with the observation that for
shopkeepers and prostitutes these lean years were proving
to be years of plenty. Len was encouraged to view himself
as a vulture picking at the carcass of his wounded country.
I returned to the village alone. To face their accusing eyes.
I had not 'stuck by him'. It was now important for me to
abandon any vanity. To learn to ignore whatever they might
be saying about me. I've been training myself. In the evenings
I attend to the blackout curtains, then sit by myself and listen
to the wireless. I follow the war, listen to ITMA and read.
I often think of my mother. But I never ask her for help.

I don't ask for anybody's help. And in the shop, no matter how they look at me, I always ask them for their coupons. I wonder if they realize that if the inspectors hadn't have taken Len, then the services were about ready to take me. I was about to be classified 'mobile', as they're getting desperate. My invalid husband would have just had to learn how to look after himself. As he will have to when he gets out.

APRIL 1943

He came on the Sunday morning that I go down to visit my mother. The first Sunday morning of each month. He was dressed smartly in his uniform and he was carrying yet more daffodils. I've brought you some more of these yellow flowers. I like how they look. I smiled. Once again, I left him in the front of the shop while I went around the back to find a jar. I saw the ring that I'd taken off and put by the kitchen tap. My God, what was I doing? There was something brassy about having taken it off and not having replaced it. But I didn't care. I left the ring there, jammed the flowers into a jar, and came back through into the shop. I didn't know if I should bring you some candy, he said. But it doesn't matter. I can let you have some whenever you want. All you have to do is say when. He seemed nervous, so I touched him on the arm. That's all right, I said. Don't worry. Let's go. I smiled at him and he seemed to relax a little. For a walk? Not exactly, I said. I thought we could go and see my mother. His face dropped. It's all right, I said. She's dead. He didn't know what to do. I tell you what. I'll take the flowers, if that's all right with you. We can put them on the grave. Then he started to laugh, and I realized that it would be all right. My mother used to like flowers, I said. I took them out of the jar. We waited at the bus stop. People passed by on their way to church. It was nothing to do with him. They didn't talk to me anyhow. I wondered if there was some way of letting him know this. That it wasn't anything to do with him why they weren't talking. But I decided that it was too early to tell him this. I might as well let him work some things out for himself. We talked on the bus. Most of the time I just listened, for he talked more than I did. He told me a bit about himself, and why he joined the army. Me, I didn't like to ask too much because I don't know much about Americans. Or Coloureds. I was sure that I was going to make a mistake. Bound to. So I said nothing. I just kept my mouth shut and listened to him talking to me in that sing-song accent of his. I like it. It makes me laugh, although I'm not sure that it's supposed to. The way he stretches out words. When we got to town we went straight to the cemetery and he was very proper. I let him put the flowers on my mother. He asked me if I wanted to say a prayer. I looked at him, unsure as to what to do. I thought I'd better just tell the truth. I don't know any prayers, I said. This wasn't really true. I do know some, but I'm not very good at such things. Like prayers. He said that was all right, but would I mind if he said one. I said, course not. So he did. When it was over, I thought that I'd better tell him that there's not really that much to see and do in the town. That's the honest truth. I don't care what anybody says. It's not really any place to show a visitor. He suggested that we could talk as we walked the streets, so we did. And again we talked about him, and I tried to avoid the way people were looking. They were looking at me. Not him. They just nodded at him. Some people asked him for a Lucky Strike. He always gave away two, and a smile. I thought that was nice. It made me think nice things about him. But nobody would say anything to me. I knew what they were thinking. That he was just using me for fun. There was no ring on my finger, but I didn't think that they had the right to look at me in that way. Just who the hell did they think they were? I told my friend that I thought we should sit down in the park for a minute. I didn't feel all that well. In fact, I told him, I felt a bit dizzy. He wrapped his finger and thumb around my wrist. You sure you're getting enough to eat? Yes, thank you. You sure you don't want me to fix you up with some Hershey bars? I smiled. We sat awkwardly and in silence, he with his thoughts, I with mine. I just kept thinking, I can't see what they're getting out of it. Being so cruel. But I was just making myself more and more angry, and I could sense that it was getting difficult for him. I slipped my arm inside his and asked him if he fancied going to the pictures. He smiled. Sure, why not? And so there we were, in the dark in the Elektra Palace, watching the first house, but I wasn't really watching, and I sensed that he could tell. I felt such a fool, but I didn't know how to tell him that it wasn't his fault. That it was nothing to do with him. Honestly. When we came out it was dark and I knew we'd missed the bus. I didn't know what to do. We walked aimlessly towards the bus stop and then I realized that I'd better own up. He looked at his watch. I've got to be back in an hour. Surely there's some other way? What about a taxi? I told him that I'd never taken a taxi. I didn't know if they still ran, what with the blackout and everything. Then I told him that I was sorry. That I didn't want to get him into trouble. He looked at me. Don't worry. It's not your fault. I knew he wasn't telling me the truth. He was trying to spare my feelings. We stood and waited for an imaginary taxi. Small 'starlight' bulbs have now replaced all the standard ones. These bulbs cast faintly illuminated circles down on to the pavement, which is supposed to make it easier for us to see. I explained to him that apparently you can't see these lights from above. He touched my arm. I could see that he was worried. After half an hour, he flagged down a military jeep. MPs, he whispered. We both climbed into the back of the jeep. He told them I'd been kind enough to introduce him to my mother. Then she got sick and we had to wait on her. I wanted to laugh, but I was frightened. The two men in the front of the jeep said nothing. And I knew now that I had got him into big trouble. I wanted the earth to swallow me up. He laced his hands around his knees and we rode back in silence.

APRIL 1943

Last night I dreamed about the matinée we saw last Sunday afternoon. Not the actual film, because I hardly watched that. But a different film. In fact, it was like a different day altogether. The film was about a soldier on leave who meets a squire's daughter. Her toffee-nosed father is a veteran of the 1914–18 war. He's not sure about this young whipper-snapper walking out with his daughter, but slowly he comes to realize that he's not a bad lad. And the young soldier is won over when he realizes that the old boy goes firewatching with the local yokels. In other words, he does his bit. I hated the film because it didn't tell the truth, but my friend quite liked it. He told me that this was his first English film. Afterwards, I took him for fish and chips, then we got the bus home. When I woke up, I thought I was going to cry.

MAY 1943

I hadn't seen him in nearly three weeks now, so I decided
that the next time one of the soldiers came into the shop,
I'd gather up my courage and ask him about my friend. And
then this morning the officer with the dark glasses, Mr Hello,
Duchess, he popped in to ask the way to some place or other.
After I'd told him what he wanted to know, I asked him if
my friend was being punished. At first he looked surprised,
then he just said, yes. I told him that this was unfair, and
that what had happened was no fault of my friend's. But the
officer pretended that he didn't hear me. He smiled, saluted,
and then turned on his heels and left. I closed the shop early
and began the short walk down to the camp. I went up to the
soldiers on the gate. They asked me what I wanted, but I just
told them that I wanted to see the man in charge and they did
nothing after that. They just stood to one side and I walked
right through. I went up to the main office and was shown
into a room where a man was sitting behind a desk. Yes,
he snapped. Then, after he looked up and saw who it was
standing in front of him, he stood up and extended a hand.
I'm sorry. Please take a seat. I looked at him but continued
to stand. He sat down. My friend, I said. He's being punished
for something that's not his fault. He furrowed his brow as if
he didn't quite know whom it was I was referring to. Your
friend? I wasn't about to play this game. I stared right back at
him. He knew who my friend was. I went on and explained
how it was my fault that we missed the bus. How I was the
one, if anybody, who should be blamed. He then started to

tell me about discipline. And how important it was in the army that orders were obeyed. And that if you made an exception for one, you soon found that you had to make an exception for everybody. I listened. And then I explained again that it was my fault that we missed the bus. He looked at me. What would you like me to do about it? Believe me, I said. The bloody little squirt looked back down at his desk. I'll see what I can do, he said. Which really meant nothing, for we both knew he could do whatever he wanted to do. I turned and started to leave. But it's not that we don't want our men to mix with you village girls, it's not that at all. It's just that we don't want any incidents. It hasn't been easy for any of us. I turned and walked out of the door. Walking back across the camp, I had the feeling that everybody knew who I was, and that they knew why I'd been to see the commanding officer. I wandered back up towards the shop. Some villagers stopped and stared at me. They pointed by simply nodding their heads in my direction. Both inside the camp, and outside, I was attracting attention. But for the wrong reasons.

JUNE 1943

Today he came into the shop. I couldn't help myself, I let out a little scream of delight. He didn't want to buy anything. He just wanted to talk. He told me how embarrassed he'd been in the back of the jeep. I said that he had no reason to be embarrassed. After all, I was the one who should be embarrassed. I was the one who'd got us into the mess to start with. I said, If I'd been keeping a check on the time then it would never have happened in the first place. We fought over this and then fell silent when an old woman came in for her fags. She looked in the direction of my friend, but said nothing beyond 'ta' as she left. For a while the noise of the doorbell echoed in the silence. It registered a change of tone for the whole conversation. My friend lowered his voice and said how grateful he was that I had taken the trouble to come and help him out. I decided to close up the shop. Well, it was almost time anyway. I turned the sign around and drew the latch. Once I'd done this he relaxed. He told me that the military police hadn't taken him back to the camp. After they dropped me off, they'd driven him down the road to a clearing and told him to get out of the jeep. And then they beat him with their sticks. He said they beat him so hard that he thought his kidneys were going to burst. I closed my mouth, which I now realized had been hanging open. When they took him back to the camp, they'd made a report that said that he'd been drunk and difficult. As a result, the commanding officer had decided that he was to be confined to the camp until further notice. I was horrified when he told me this, but he seemed to take it as a matter of course. He told me that the army only liked to use them for cleaning and the like. I asked him if he'd like to come to the pub with me for a drink. I wanted him to continue talking to me. I wanted him to try to understand that I needed to know more about him, otherwise I would keep getting upset and just make more mistakes. I was bound to if I didn't get any help. He asked me if I thought it was proper that he should go into the pub with me. I looked at him and told him that there was nothing wrong with his going into the pub with me. Why should there be? Fine, then we'll go to the pub, he said. I locked the door behind us. I noticed that there was nobody on the streets. I expected everybody was having their tea. It was that time of the day. And in the pub, there was just the odd old boy. Nobody, really. He ordered a pint and a half of bitter. The landlord liked them. The Americans. I think he had a soft spot for them, wanted them to feel at home. And once they realized that the beer was always going to taste flat and warm, and that sometimes you would have to drink out of a jar if he ran out of glasses, then they were all right about everything. He even laughed when one of them handed him back a pint and told him to pour it back into the horse that it came from. And I liked the landlord. I'd noticed that after he'd been in the cellar to tap a new cask, he had a habit of taking a quiet smoke in the back parlour, as opposed to the public bar. It was as though he needed time to himself to collect his thoughts. I liked that about him. And then he'd come through into the public and knock out his empty pipe. Travis brought the pint and a half over to the seat in the corner. I told him that from here we'd soon be able to watch the sun go down.

JUNE 1943

Once back at the shop, he sat with me upstairs. And I offered him tea. Hot tea, as he insisted on calling it. And he said very little. It had already been said. I asked him if he was hungry, but he just shook his head. I'm not much of a cook, so that solved that. I realized that he probably didn't want to listen to the wireless, and I couldn't blame him. So we were happy with the silence, and the occasional comment. It wasn't too difficult or too awkward. If we had something to say, it was said. And that was the end of it. It grew dark outside. There was no noise, as ever. Across the room I saw the framed photograph of Len and me on our wedding day. Turned down. Its face buried in a thin layer of dust on top of the chest of drawers. And then Travis got to his feet. I have to go now. I have to get back. I'm sorry if I've taken up too much of your time. I just wanted to say thank you. Did I ever – he changes tack now – did I ever show you pictures of my home town? Or pictures of my folks? He must know that he never did. It's not the type of thing that a man would do for a virtual stranger and then forget about. And certainly not this man. I was already sure of that. No, I said. But I would love to see them. Okay, he said. I'll bring them along. Next time. He saluted. I laughed. And then he reached out his hand for me to shake. I'll walk back with you, I said. He gave a little laugh, as though nervous. Now don't you worry, he said. Little danger of my getting lost. Although, never know who you're gonna run into on the roads. Military Police. Anyone. His hand was beginning to look foolish, so I took it and held it between both of mine. And I surprised myself, for I squeezed it. Gently. Then he leaned forward and kissed my hand. Thank you, I said. Thank you, he said. The lights were out. I could see his eyes gleaming. He wrestled his hand out from between mine. I wanted to catch it like a slippery fish, but he was too nimble for me. I have to go now, he said. I'll be fine by myself. I'm sorry. I smiled. I knew he meant it. I knew he did. He was sorry that he had to go. After I closed the door behind him, I went back upstairs. I picked up the cup and saucer that he had been drinking out of, and I ran my finger around the rim of the cup. A little tea stain. And then I saw the mark in the settee where he'd been sitting. The room smelt of him. A good smell. I could smell him on me. I wasn't going to be alone again. As long as I didn't open any windows or doors. As long as I didn't wash anything. Then I could make the smell last a little longer.

JULY 1943

Yesterday they arrested Mussolini. The BBC announcer said
that Hitler's 'utensil' had fallen off the Axis shelf. I was sitting
in the pub by myself when the news came through. The
landlord got out the monthly ration of whisky to celebrate
what he said looked like the end. He offered me some, but I
said no. Then he said that the Yanks would probably have to
go over to Italy to clean up. He said he'd miss them. I felt a
door closing inside of me. I looked up at him. He asked me
again if I wanted a whisky. I nodded. He knew what he'd said.
At least I have to give him that. It was still bright out, so I
walked home the long way round to give myself some time
to think. As I passed the church hall it occurred to me just how
difficult it is to come by cosmetics, nail files, hair grips and the
like. I'd never had much reason to fret over them before. Such
things had never mattered. But now I found myself thinking
that I could kill for a bar of scented soap.

JULY 1943

There are some girls from the town who seem to have no shame. Some factory girls, some plain common tarts, mainly bottle-blondes, all of them with legs like Grecian columns. They've started to frequent the camp. Apparently, some of them even spend the night there, and they go far beyond furtive clutching. He told me that nylons, nail varnish, perfume and the like, all these things that they can get from the PX, this stuff is known to them as 'shack-up' material. He said this is why he'd never offered me any, but clearly his mates weren't so fussy. It appears that some girls will do anything for goods or provisions. Since soap and sweets went on coupons, things must have got worse. I heard a woman in the shop today saying that there are some of them up there at the camp who'll let loose for a fresh orange. She went on. After all, you can only eat so much Spam. She said, These days sex is about the only thing that isn't rationed. She reckoned that this went some way towards accounting for the diseases that they say are going around.

DECEMBER 1943

Len came back today. He told me that he still loves me. He'd had time to think things over. I might not realize it yet, but the truth was that in spite of everything, he couldn't help himself, he loved me. I liked that. In spite of everything. Bloody charming. That made me feel really wanted. But I didn't say anything. I just looked at him standing in front of me, looking around his kingdom. He didn't have to say anything. I knew what he was thinking. I knew what he felt about me being in his place. But I wasn't going anywhere. He could look all he wanted to, but this was also my place now. He wanted to say something. I wanted him to say it. But he said nothing. So I spoke. Len, I said. I don't want to live with you as man and wife. What do you mean? His look said that. Nothing else. Just, what do you mean? I mean, one of us will be sleeping on the settee in future. I don't really mind who. I don't care. Len sat down. In fact, he half sat, half collapsed. Then he began. I hear there's talk about you and an American. I knew there would be talk. In fact – I shouldn't say this – I had been hoping that Len might find out. I knew it was cruel. But what could I do? It's how I felt. I was hoping that I wouldn't have to find some awkward way of telling him. Yes, I've got a friend, I said. Now it was my turn to sit. I faced him, and passed him the torch of conversation. He could say whatever he wanted to say. And so he did. I don't think you should have friends like that. It makes a bloody fool out of me. I laughed. And getting put inside. Getting yourself carted off to jail doesn't make me look like a bloody fool, is that it? Len stood up. He pushed his finger into my face. He jabbed at me to punctuate his sentences. You won't see him, or any of 'em. You won't go to town, to the pub, have them in here, talk to them, nothing, as long as I'm here. I'd never have married you, or taken you out of that bloody slum, if I'd known you were going to behave like a slut. Now am I making myself clear? Yes, Len, I say. You're making yourself perfectly clear. But I won't have any of it. It's not for me to say what you do, any more than it is for you to talk to me in this way. His poor jaw dropped. I'm your bloody husband. Yes, I said. You're my bloody husband. In name only. His fist caught me across the left side of my face. I could feel the swelling right away. As though somebody was puffing up my face like a balloon. And then he kicked me in the stomach and I doubled up. I'm your bloody husband whether you like it or not. Not in name, you slut. In fact. In law and in fact. Now, like I told you. We're leaving. I've got work north of here. We're selling the shop. It's half mine, I gasped. And we're not selling. I didn't see why I should have to bother with this conversation. So I said nothing further. We're leaving, said Len. I remained silent. Do you hear? A piece of coal fell, and for a few seconds the fire blazed as the unburned coal caught. It made a crackling, definite noise. We both stared at the fire. For a moment we were caught by its performance. Then we looked at each other. I knew he wouldn't touch me again. He'd made his point. And then there was the shame. I suspect there's always a certain amount of shame involved for all men. After they've thrown the punch. They look and see you cowering. And the thought crosses their mind that perhaps they ought not to have done this. That perhaps this is not a proper way to hold a conversation. They're sorry. It's pitiful. I looked at him and dared him to continue to talk to me. I dared him to hit me again. But he wouldn't. I knew this, but I taunted him with my silence until he left for the pub.

DECEMBER 1943

Half an hour after he left, it became clear to me what I should do. I pulled on my coat. I was in a hurry. I closed in the door behind me and began to walk briskly towards the pub. I looked up. The moon was wrapped in a thick and heavy fog, and I was cold so I started to run. It was Friday night and I was sure that they would all be there. I was sure of it. I opened the door to the pub and all eyes were on me. I walked in and stopped. The place was full. My heart was pounding away and I couldn't catch my breath. Len saw me. He frowned. He might as well just look on, I thought, because I'm in the pub and I'm not going anywhere. He was sitting in the corner with his friends. So I went over and sat next to him. I think he must have already realized that the strange man in the pub was my husband. But he didn't do anything. Except reach up and touch my face. What happened? I didn't say anything. I just looked across at Len. Why? Now I looked back at Travis. His friends fired questions. Her old man beat her up? Because of you, man? They tried to ask without making things uncomfortable for me. Then they remembered. One of them asked me if I'd like a drink. Like a drink, Joyce? I don't think I do. This is what I said. That I didn't think I did, thank you. And so I waited for a while. But I could see that I was making them uneasy. I got up and decided to go. Travis stood and said that he would walk with me. No, I said. Again I glanced purposefully at the husband. Then I left. Before I did so, I touched his hand. I just wanted you to know. These were my parting words. But know what? I thought.

FEBRUARY 1944

Len was drunk. That's not something I have to remember. Len
was usually drunk. His arms and legs were moving at the same
time. Like a machine. He made big circles and small circles.
And like a machine Len struck every time. And then suddenly
he was there, pulling Len away. He knocked him down with
a punch. I watched Len's mouth open and close, and these
words. These ugly words coming from my husband. Len
climbed to his feet, but again he was knocked to the ground.
And then two more soldiers. His friends. They were trying to
hold back the man who had rescued me. They were saying,
no. Enough. Travis was holding Len by the throat. Len had
fear in his eyes. Travis told him that if he ever laid a finger
on me again, then he would be found somewhere in a ditch
with an American bullet in him. Len had to be brave, so he
continued to spit out his ugly words. But it was not really
bravery. He just wanted to look brave. That was Len. But he
wouldn't say anything to me. He didn't care enough about me
to actually say anything to me. My friend. He is my friend.
Maybe he cares too much. I didn't feel I deserved this. To be
rescued like this. Truly. To me it seemed strange.

MARCH 1944

Len has gone to his new job in the north. He's said I can have
the divorce. No point in squabbling about it. He reckons we
should be able to get a special quick one, what with him having
a record and everything. In the meantime, I'm to run the shop.
He asked me if I would. I said yes. After the war he says he'll
come back. If I decide to leave before the war's over, I'm to let
him know. He'll sell the shop. But meanwhile he gets a share
of the profits. That's Len's way. There's always something
in it for him. Before he left he told me that I'm a traitor to
my own kind. That as far as he's concerned I'm no better
than a common slut. And everybody in the village agrees
with him.

JULY 1944

Today I checked to make sure. I was right. Pregnant women get extra concentrated orange juice. An extra pint of milk a day. An extra half-ration of meat a week. An extra egg (up to three a week). Free cod-liver oil. Free chocolate-covered vitamin tablets. And a baby.

8 MAY 1945

Today's the day that everyone's been waiting for, but it's all confused. It's over, but it's not official. We know now that there will be no more sirens, searchlights, or blackouts. But somebody has to make it official. I spent the whole evening looking out of the window. At about ten o'clock, people began to give up and drift back inside. The street party will have to wait. Greer slept through all the excitement. Up above, the light, damp clouds have now begun to swell. It will bucket down all night.

9 MAY 1945

Churchill spoke at three p.m. He called it the people's victory, but we all knew it was his. Churchill's. At the end of his speech, there was loud cheering. Everybody spilled out into the street to enjoy the two days of holiday. The bunting meant something now, as did the Union Jacks and the portraits of Winnie. We had won the war. I put my hair up in a wrap and stepped out to join them. I held Greer and watched as they put on hats and sang. Then they danced the hokey-cokey and swilled down dandelion and burdock and ginger beer. I'd done my bit. I'd supplied them with their food. Some went off to church. The bells were ringing again. I hoped that at least one of them might remember Sandra. Others lit a bonfire, and on to it went army forms, and ration books; anything to do with the war. And there was a crude effigy of Hitler. That burned quickly. At nine p.m., the King made a speech in his usual stammer. I'd never had much time for these people, but it was moving. Some of them even spoke to me and smiled at Greer. Just before midnight, I took him inside, out of the evening chill.

2

1963

It was nearly four o'clock. I stared at Greer and longed for him
to stay as dearly as I longed for him to leave. I'd explained that
I thought he should go before the children came back. He said
he understood. The silences had become more awkward, but
at least they remained free of accusation. A handsome man.
Yes, a man. No longer a baby. Or a boy. He got to his feet.
I knew he would never call me mother. He could go, but
would he come back? It wasn't for me to ask him. I hadn't
asked him here in the first place. For eighteen years I hadn't
invited him to do anything. Not since the lady with the blue
coat and maroon scarf. With her tiny dog named Monty. She
was so wet you could pour her into a jug. My GI baby. No
father, no mother, no Uncle Sam. It must go into the care *abandonment*.
of the County Council as an orphan, love. If you're lucky, it
might be legally adopted into a well-to-do family. Some are,
you know. For weeks afterwards I wandered around the park
looking at women pushing their prams. Their awkward babies
screamed as though they'd tumbled straight from the womb
and into these contraptions. For eighteen years I hadn't invited
Greer to do anything. Your father and I, Greer. We couldn't
show off. We had to be careful. And bold. We started a dance
once. My God, I remember that. And for weeks afterwards,
every time I thought of him I was sure my knees were going
to give way. Then, later, they took him away from me, to
Italy. I'd go to the cinema in the hope of seeing him. But they
just showed the Tommies. Never the Yanks. And if they did,
never the Coloureds. I once got two letters from him on the

same day, and I didn't know which one to open first. And then he came back on New Year's Day, 1945. For the wedding. And now, I don't even have a picture of him. I'm sorry, love. I destroyed everything. Letters, pictures, everything. When I met Alan. It seemed the right thing to do, but I was stupid. He spoke again. I'd better go now, he said. My God, I wanted to hug him. I wanted him to know that I did have feelings for him. Both then and now. He was my son. Our son.

NEW YEAR'S DAY, 1945

He came back on compassionate leave. The doctor had said
I was having a breakdown and a baby. Just seventy-two
hours, that's all they'd given him, then he'd have to go
back. I went down to town to meet him, but I nearly
wept when I saw him getting off the train. He looked as
thin as a door, and so tired. He didn't have that bounce
in his step. He didn't have any joy in his face. Everybody
stared at him. I think they must have felt sorry for him,
bending under the weight of that bag on his back. He
looked like the saddest man in the world. Even before I'd
fallen pregnant, he'd asked me if we could get wed. At
first I thought it was only the war talking, but eventually
I told him yes, as soon as I was rid of Len. Maybe I was
a bit worried that he'd leave me behind after the war. He'd
already told me that we couldn't live together in America.
It wouldn't be allowed. I thought getting wed would be
a way of keeping him here. In England. As he walked
towards me along the black length of the platform, with
that slow stride and those hunched shoulders, I could see
just how shattered he was. He had huge bags under his
eyes, and he hadn't shaved for days. And then he saw
me, and the child pushing at my coat. He stopped and
stared. I could feel myself colouring over. And then he
came right up to me, and I started to cry. The doctor
was right, my nerves wanted building up. He let his bag
fall to the platform. Joyce. That was all he said. Just, Joyce.
I could see now, the gap in the middle of his teeth. At the

bottom. And then he reached out and pulled me towards him. I couldn't believe it. He'd come back to me. He really wanted me. That day, crying on the platform, safe in Travis's arms.

1945

I stood there in that freezing room, the eyes of the two unknown witnesses staring at my back, Travis at my side, my belly out in front of me, wishing the Registrar would just hurry it up a bit. He had this thin smile painted across his mouth, and there was something about him that I truly disliked. When I came to make the appointment, he told me that he'd done one other GI bride's wedding. I didn't tell him that he'd not have done one like this, though. After the divorce came through, I'd written to Travis in Italy and told him. He wrote back and told me that he'd got his commanding officer's permission, as long as he didn't try and take me back to America with him. They weren't having any of that. Me, I wasn't right over there. After I got his letter, I went to the Registrar and made an appointment. He told me that he'd done one other GI bride's wedding.

1945

Nobody said anything, but when they lifted him clear of my body and began to towel him down, I knew what they were thinking. I stared at him. My beautiful son. The nurse placed him in my arms. He's like coffee, isn't he, love. I had no idea then that his father would never see him. Later, after I'd got the telegram, after the war was over, the lady with the blue coat came to visit. I could see her looking at me and thinking, poor disillusioned cow. You'll be better off, love, with somebody else looking after him. Trust me. I know what I'm on about. I mean, how are you going to cope? You won't know what to do now, will you. Let's be sensible. You're going to have to start a new life on your own. And so we were sensible, my son and I. My son who hadn't asked me to turn him over to the lady with the blue coat and maroon scarf.

1945

The Red Cross man knocked once. Then again, impatiently. Hardly gave me time to set Greer right and get down the stairs. I opened the door and he handed me the telegram. I didn't have a chance to say much of anything. He just smiled slightly and began to back away. I closed in the door. The telegram didn't say much. I had to try to imagine it. To die at first light on the Italian coast. Fear. Mud. Shivering cold. Noise. Silence louder than any noise. Mortar fire. A bullet. A young man screaming in pain, shouting out for mercy to a God he no longer believed existed. His flesh ripped open by hot, flying metal. A man with blood flowing like red wine from his open veins. In a strange country. Among people he hardly knew. I remembered what my mother had said to me when I told her that I was getting married. At least you're not getting wed to a soldier, she'd said. You should never do that, for you'll just be left on your own. I closed the shop. I didn't open up for three days. On the second day, two of them came to see me. They'd heard. They asked me if there was anything they could do. No, I said. Thank you, but no. After the telegram, I tried not to be angry. I knew everything was going on around me like normal. People were still having their usual at the pub. They were still going off to work the next morning. I was the only one who'd lost anything. They'd lost nothing. Just been inconvenienced a bit by this war. We hadn't even been bombed in this bloody stupid village. I wanted to break something. I really wanted to smash something to bits. The following month it was all over. I put my hair up in a wrap and stepped out to join them. I held Greer and watched as they put on hats and sang. Then they danced the hokey-cokey. I'd done my bit. I'd supplied them with their food. Some went off to church. The bells were ringing again. I hoped that at least one of them might remember Sandra. Others lit a bonfire, and on to it went army forms and ration books; anything to do with the war. And there was a crude effigy of Hitler. That burned quickly. At nine p.m. the King made a speech in his usual stammer. I'd never had much time for these people, but it was moving. Some of them even spoke to me and smiled at Greer. Just before midnight, I took him inside, out of the evening chill. A week later she turned up. The lady with the blue coat. With her dog, Monty. And Len was back. He wanted his shop. I had no money. Nothing. Only Greer. She said, You're going to have to start a new life on your own. And so we were sensible, my son and I. Into the care of the County Council as an orphan, love. It hadn't really dawned on me, but it was true. His father would never see him. Never. I left the village, the shop, my ex-husband, and went to live back in the town. On my own. For weeks afterwards, I wandered around the park looking at women pushing their prams.

1963

I was in the kitchen, wringing out clothes in the sink. I happened to glance up. I saw him, standing at the front gate. I knew that it was him. I knew that one day he would come looking. That he would find me. I could hear myself breathing. But apart from this, I was calm. I surprised myself. He had a piece of paper in his hand that he kept glancing at. Then he'd look back up at the house, then back down at the paper. Then he pushed the paper into his pocket. Alan was at work, and the kids wouldn't be back from school until four o'clock. The first thing that occurred to me was that he'd chosen his time well. That maybe he'd planned it all right down to the last detail. I looked at his hair. It was too short to be styled into that greasy Teddy Boy look. I hated that look. He unlatched the gate and began to walk up the path. I wasn't going to be able to pretend that I wasn't in. I waited until he'd knocked once. Then when he knocked a second time I went to the door and opened it. We stood and looked at each other, me drying my hands on a tea towel. My God, he was handsome. Come in. He seemed shy. Come in, come in. He stepped by me, dipping a shoulder as he did so in order that we didn't have to touch. I closed in the door but for a moment I didn't turn around. I was ashamed. I wasn't ready. Standing there in a plain dress, with my lank hair, and my bare legs, and my slippers looking like the left-over scraps from somebody's fluffy rug. Forty-five years old, and I knew I looked awful, but there wasn't any time to fret over appearances. Not now. I took a deep breath and turned to face him. I almost said make yourself at home, but I didn't. At least I avoided that. Sit down. Please, sit down.

I hear a drum beating on the far bank of the river. A breeze stirs and catches it. The resonant pounding is borne on the wind, carried high above the roof-tops, across the water, above the hinterland, high above the tree-tops, before its beat plunges down and into the interior. I wait. And then listen as the many-tongued chorus of the common memory begins again to swell, and insist that I acknowledge greetings from those who lever pints of ale in the pubs of London. Receive salutations from those who submit to (what the French call) neurotic inter-racial urges in the boulevards of Paris. ('No first-class nation can afford to produce a race of mongrels.') But my Joyce, and my other children, their voices hurt but determined, they will survive the hardships of the far bank. Only if they panic will they break their wrists and ankles against Captain Hamilton's instruments. *Put 2 in irons and delicately in the thumbscrews to encourage them to a full confession of those principally involved. In the evening put 5 more in neck-yokes.* Survivors all. In Brooklyn a helplessly addicted mother waits for the mist to clear from her eyes. They have stopped her benefit. She lives now without the comfort of religion, electricity, or money. A barefoot boy in São Paulo is rooted to his piece of the earth, which he knows will never swell up, pregnant, and become a vantage point from which he will be able to see beyond his dying *favela*. In Santo Domingo, a child suffers the hateful hot comb, the dark half-moons of history heavy beneath each eye. A mother watches. Her eleven-year-old daughter is preparing herself for yet another night of premature prostitution. Survivors. In their diasporan souls a dream like steel. *I praise His holy name that I was fortunate enough to be born in a Christian country, amongst Christian parents and friends, and that you were kind enough to take me, a foolish child, from my parents and bring me up in your own dwelling as something more akin to son than servant. Truth and honesty is great capital, and you instilled such values in my person at an early age, for which I am eternally grateful to you and my Creator.* Enduring cities which whisper falsehoods through perfectly shaped wooden lips. *A dream began to wash through her mind. Martha dreamed that she had travelled on west to California, by herself, and clutching her bundle of clothing. Once there she was met by Eliza Mae, who was now a tall, sturdy colored woman of some social standing. Together, they tip-toed their way through the mire of the streets to Eliza Mae's residence, which stood on a fine, broad avenue.* For two hundred and fifty years I have listened. To voices in the streets of Charleston. (The slave who mounted this block is now dying young from copping a fix on some rusty needle in an Oakland project.) I have listened. To reggae rhythms of rebellion and revolution dipping through the hills and valleys of the Caribbean. I have listened. To the saxophone player on a wintry night in Stockholm. A long way from home. For two hundred and fifty years I have listened. To my Nash. My Martha. My Travis. *Joyce. That was all he said. Just, Joyce. I could see now the gap in the middle of his teeth. At the bottom. And then he reached out and pulled me towards him. I couldn't believe it. He'd come back to me. He really wanted me. That day, crying on the platform, safe in Travis's arms.* For two hundred and fifty years I have listened. To the haunting voices. Singing: Mercy, Mercy Me. (The Ecology.) Insisting: Man, I ain't got no quarrel with them Vietcong. Declaring: Brothers and Friends. I am Toussaint L'Ouverture, my name is perhaps known to you. Listened to: Papa Doc. Baby Doc. Listened to voices hoping for: Freedom. Democracy. Singing: Baby, baby. Where did our love go? Samba. Calypso. Jazz. Jazz. Sketches of Spain in Harlem. In a Parisian bookstore a voice murmurs the words.

Nobody Knows My Name. I have listened to the voice that cried: I have a dream that one day on the red hills of Georgia, the sons of former slaves and the sons of former slave-owners will be able to sit down together at the table of brotherhood. I have listened to the sounds of an African carnival in Trinidad. In Rio. In New Orleans. On the far bank of the river, a drum continues to be beaten. A many-tongued chorus continues to swell. And I hope that amongst these survivors' voices I might occasionally hear those of my own children. My Nash. My Martha. My Travis. My daughter. Joyce. All. Hurt but determined. Only if they panic will they break their wrists and ankles against Captain Hamilton's instruments. A guilty father. Always listening. There are no paths in water. No signposts. There is no return. A desperate foolishness. The crops failed. I sold my beloved children. *Bought 2 strong man-boys, and a proud girl.* But they arrived on the far bank of the river, loved.

BOOKS BY CARYL PHILLIPS

"[Phillips is] a master ventriloquist, giving immediacy and voice to an impressive range of vivid characters."   —*San Francisco Chronicle*

CAMBRIDGE

A prim and increasingly apprehensive Englishwoman observing the peculiarities of a sugar plantation in the nineteenth-century West Indies. A devout black slave whose profoundly Christian sense of justice is about to cost him his life. In *Cambridge*, Phillips creates a suspenseful and inescapably damning portrait of the schizophrenia of slavery.

Fiction/Literature/0-679-73689-1

CROSSING THE RIVER

This novel, shortlisted for the Booker Prize, begins in Africa in a year of failing crops and desperate foolishness, which forces a father to sell his three children into slavery. Phillips follows these exiles—including a freed slave journeying to Liberia, a pioneer woman seeking refuge from the white man's justice on the Colorado frontier, and an African-American G.I. who falls in love with a white woman during World War II—across the river that separates continents and centuries, giving us one of the most stunning works of fiction ever to address the lives of black people severed from their homeland.

Fiction/Literature/0-679-75794-5

HIGHER GROUND

In this searing novel about slavery and its legacy, Phillips tells multiple stories, set generations and continents apart but unified by their ambitious exploration of themes of race, power, captivity, and abuse. These narratives take on a devastating power, confirming his reputation as a writer who understands the stranglehold the past exercises on the present.

Fiction/Literature/0-679-76376-7

ALSO AVAILABLE:
The Final Passage, 0-679-75931-X
A State of Independence, 0-679-75930-1

VINTAGE INTERNATIONAL
Available at your local bookstore, or call toll-free to order:
1-800-793-2665 (credit cards only).

VINTAGE INTERNATIONAL

FLAUBERT'S PARROT
by Julian Barnes

An elegant work of literary imagination involving a cranky amateur scholar's obsessive search for the truth about Gustave Flaubert, *Flaubert's Parrot* also investigates the obsession of the detective, whose passion for the page is fed by personal bitterness—and whose life seems oddly to mirror those of Flaubert's characters.

"A high literary entertainment carried off with great brio...rich in parody and parrotry, full of insight and wit...a great success."

—The New York Times Book Review

Fiction/Literature/0-679-73136-9

POSSESSION
by A. S. Byatt

An intellectual mystery and a triumphant love story of a pair of young scholars researching the lives of two Victorian poets.

"A masterpiece of wordplay and adventure, a novel that compares with Stendhal and Joyce."   *—The Washington Post Book World*

Winner of the Booker Prize
Fiction/Literature/0-679-73590-9

THE STRANGER
by Albert Camus

Through the story of an ordinary man who unwittingly gets drawn into a senseless murder, Camus explores what he termed "the nakedness of man faced with the absurd."

Fiction/Literature/0-679-72020-0

INVISIBLE MAN
by Ralph Ellison

This searing record of a black man's journey through contemporary America reveals, in Ralph Ellison's words, "the sheer rhetorical challenge involved in communicating across our barriers of race and religion, class, color and region."

"The greatest American novel in the second half of the twentieth century...the classic representation of American black experience."   —R.W. B. Lewis

Fiction/Literature/0-679-72313-7